A NICE PIECE OF FLYING

A NICE PIECE OF FLYING

Stories of War, Memory, and Coming Home

ROBERT J. FLOOD

Edited by Kevin Flood

ISBN: 979-8-9942955-0-2 (Hardcover)
ISBN: 979-8-9942955-1-9 (Paperback)
ISBN: 979-8-9942955-2-6 (eBook)

Book cover and interior design by Theo Orion

IMAGE CREDITS

The cover and interior artworks are composed of multiple images.
All images have been modified (cropped, layered, color-adjusted, and combined).

Images requiring attribution:

- *Bright light on black background* – Freepik, used under Freepik License.
- *Grunge photo frame edges with distressed strokes* – Freepik, used under Freepik License.
- *Letter from William Henry Warner (WWI Soldier) to his parents – April 1915* – Wikimedia Commons, CC BY-SA 2.0.
- *World War II vintage newspaper* – Wikimedia Commons, CC BY-SA 2.0.

Public domain images:
Additional images used in the cover and interior are from Unsplash, Wikimedia Commons, Picryl, the Library of Congress, and Rawpixel.

My brother, Brian, and I are grateful to our all-in colleagues who helped make this book possible.

Kahlilah Hammond turned original typewritten pages and onion skins into Word documents.

Melissa Culverwell brought a deft, insightful editing touch to these stories. She helped keep Bob Flood's voice intact.

Liz Dubelman got us over the finish line. She brought fresh eyes, insight, and a passion for the book that made the difference.

Their all-in participation helped make this book possible.
We are in your debt.

CONTENTS

FOREWORD

Robert Flood (1921–2001) wrote these five stories from the late 1970s through the early 1980s. It was one way of dealing with what was left inside thirty-some years after WWII.

It took a while for him to make useful sense of what had happened. The stories in *A Nice Piece of Flying* are rooted in Bob's real-life experience in WWII before, during, and after the war.

In "A Nice Piece of Flying," a middle-aged insurance company owner relives his pilot past when, at a county airport, he casually steals a P-51, the same model of plane he flew in combat.

"Mr. Birnbaum" looks at a child's friendship with an adult as they age and evolve. The two men encounter each other in and out of war and discover they have more in common than not.

In "The Rough and Tumble Champion of Kansas," a former Army ironworker from the South Bronx tells the story of the toughest guy he ever met.

"Christmas Tree" finds an Irish patriarch trying to maintain his hold on his daughters and his Christmas Eve traditions as boyfriends and the troubles in Europe get in the way.

In "Reunion," Michael Reilly, a former B-17 pilot, faces his anger, resentment, and POW past when he attends an Eighth Air Force reunion in Washington, D.C. Michael wants resolution when he confronts a former wing commander, now a general, whose glaring error caused Michael's plane to be shot down.

A NICE PIECE OF FLYING

A NICE PIECE OF FLYING

Charlie Billings didn't see the state police cruiser until it pulled up alongside him on Route 684. At that, the young trooper riding alone had to hit his whooper switch to get Charlie's attention. Charlie, startled by the sound, looked over at the trooper, who motioned him to move off the highway and onto the shoulder. The cruiser pulled in behind him and stopped ten yards or so from Charlie's Mercedes-Benz.

"You have a pretty heavy foot, mister," the trooper said as he beckoned Charlie out of the car into the blazing sun. "The limit is fifty-five. You were doing eighty."

"I—I wasn't aware, officer," Charlie said. "I was preoccupied." The trooper examined Charlie's driver's license and registration without responding. He walked back to his cruiser. He was perhaps a year or two older than Charlie's eldest son, Jerry. He looked tough, competent, and, Charlie decided, hard-nosed.

"Where are you going in such a hurry?" the trooper asked when he returned. "You have a clean record." He tapped the license with his finger. "It must be pretty important to take a chance on getting yourself killed."

"Nothing like that," Charlie said. "To the office is all. In White Plains. As I said, I was preoccupied. It's no excuse, I know. I've been driving for forty years, and this is only the second time I've been stopped." He raised his hands in a gesture of helplessness. The trooper looked at him narrowly.

"You alright?"

"Yes, yes," Charlie said quickly. And then "No" just as quickly. "I'm—was—so goddamn angry. Family stuff. A know-it-all son with a big mouth and a wife who always wants to start a life discussion just as I open the front door. I had 'em both this morning. First her, then him. Three hours of it. Since eight o'clock. I really don't have to go to the office. I just had to get out of the house. Just had to. I—I barely remember getting into the car." He shook his head. "Stupid. I could have killed someone."

The trooper said nothing for a few seconds. He handed Charlie back his license and registration. He lectured Charlie a bit and let him off with a warning. Charlie watched the trooper drive away, feeling both humiliated and relieved. His anger had dissipated. It was replaced by a smothering despair and confusion. He sat on the edge of the driver's seat with the door open and buried his face in his hands. Everything he had done lately—Jesus! For the past year!—seemed to spark a confrontation with either Jerry or his wife, Laura. Jerry treated him like an old guy, and Laura was convinced—and said so incessantly—that Charlie was going through the male menopause.

"You're always so grouchy," she said again and again. "You're too critical. You're pushing us away from you, out of your life."

"Sweet Christ!" he said aloud on the side of the road. "Don't they know I need them?" The sound of his own voice surprised him. He looked up to see if anyone was nearby. But he was still alone. There were few cars on the highway. He took a deep breath and moved behind the wheel. As he was about to close the door, he heard a sound that brought him out of the car again. He scanned the horizon. Over Rye Lake to the west, he saw it: a World War II P-51 Mustang. It flitted over the treetops, banked suddenly to the left, and then leveled off. Charlie could see the landing gear coming down. He watched until the aircraft disappeared behind a tree-covered rise.

"Wow!" Charlie said, and got back into the car. He moved carefully off the shoulder onto the roadway. Ten minutes later, he turned off 684 and onto the access road to Westchester County Airport. He had nothing more on his mind than to see that Mustang on the ground.

The Mustang was parked near an air service hangar well away from the main airport terminal. Charlie pulled into a parking slot marked "Visitors" outside an industrial building. He walked to the chest-high fence. The Mustang sat in the sun at the far edge of the ramp in front of the hangar. There were perhaps a dozen other craft, from tiny single-engine pleasure craft to two- and three-engine corporate jets. Without thinking much about what he was doing but aware that he might be challenged, Charlie stepped through an unlocked gate in the fence. He strode confidently amid the parked aircraft. Dressed in a business suit of obvious quality, he tried to appear as if he had the right to be in a restricted area. He was an insurance executive, and if stopped, he could say that he wanted to look at an airplane for a new insurance policy.

He reached the Mustang without incident. He stopped next to it and looked about. There wasn't a soul in sight. The doors to the hangar were closed. He checked his watch. It was a few minutes past noon. Lunchtime. That would explain the paucity of people.

The Mustang was painted in a wild design of black, yellow, white, and red. Its skin had been waxed to silky smoothness. Charlie ran his hand along its flank. Other than the paint, there was not a single thing to distinguish it from the P-51D he had flown out of England in 1944, and from fighter bases in France in '45. For all he knew, it could be the same aircraft. He had fought his share of the war in one airplane and had last seen it the day he left for his return to the States.

He stepped up on the wing root and, surprised to note that the canopy was slid back, peered into the cockpit. Dashing and smooth as the Mustang appeared on the outside, the cockpit looked as if it had not been touched. The drab olive paint had flecked off the metal surfaces. But the control stick seemed different, and the gunsight was gone. A parachute had been left on the seat, and a modern flying helmet lay atop it with earphone and microphone leads attached.

Charlie looked about, beyond the other craft and toward the service hangar. Nobody. It was uncanny, as if some force was at work protecting him from interference in what he knew now he would do. He stepped into the cockpit, picking up the helmet as he did so. The jacks for the leads were easy to locate. He sat in the seat, immersed in a cocoon of superhot air that smelled of oil-baked rubber, gasoline, and engine coolant. He had begun to sweat profusely. He buckled on the restraining straps and ran through the controls. They worked freely, which meant there were no locks on them. Wheel chocks? He hadn't looked but could not remember seeing any.

"Jesus!" he said aloud. "This is crazy! Get out now. Before it's too late." But he ticked the power switch. The instrument needles jumped to life. Fuel gauges showed half full. He flicked the starter switch. The engine was still warm from the recent flight. The huge four-bladed propeller began to turn, jerkily at first and then, as the engine roared to life, smoothly.

Charlie sensed rather than saw the three men running toward him from the direction of the hangar. Two wore mechanic coveralls. The other, young, like the trooper on the highway, wore a bright red flying suit and leather jacket. They were all waving their arms and shouting, although Charlie couldn't hear them.

Still time to shut down, get out, and face them. Tell them he meant no harm. That he just wanted to experience again that heady thrill he had known so long ago. Would they understand what that meant to a fifty-seven-year-old former fighter pilot with two and one-half kills to his credit? He advanced the throttle and tapped the brakes. No. Either way, he was in big trouble. Might as well go all the way. He held his breath. In a second, he would know whether the wheels were chocked.

The Mustang moved with the ease of a well-tuned car. Charlie felt a tightening in his stomach. He guided the Mustang off the concrete and onto the grass patch between the ramp and the runway. He did not even look back to see where the men were.

He zigzagged toward the main north–south runway, looking to see if there was anything in the pattern or on the approach. The helmet with its radio connections still lay in his lap. The runway and approaches were clear. He was on the runway; he turned, increasing power as he did so. He checked his instruments. All normal. He set his fuel mixture as if he had never stopped doing it. Everything was coming back to him. Thirty-some years ago was yesterday. There are some things you never forget.

The Mustang straightened out under full power. Charlie concentrated on the centerline of the runway. The controls felt fine, the trim was perfect. The Mustang could have flown itself off the ground. In seconds, he felt the slight "thunk" as the wheels came off the runway. He snapped the gear switch and saw in his mind's eye the wheels fold up under the wing. He held the Mustang in level flight until the end of the runway. Then he hauled the stick back and began a steep, straight-ahead climb.

He leveled off at about seven thousand feet. For the rest of his life, he would remember those few brief moments. Whatever happened when he returned to earth, it would be a price well worth paying.

He had fully intended to make a single circuit of the airport and come in. But that would be like taking a single sip of fine wine. He would finish the glass. He checked the horizon, then banked right and sped for the clear skies over Long Island Sound. Below him passed the lush greenery and the gray-black towns and villages of Westchester, where he had forged a decent, respectable, and comfortable life since he and Laura married, ten days after V-J Day. From an apartment in Yonkers to a fifteen-room home in

Pound Ridge, three cars, and an in-ground pool. He spotted the golf club, where he was a member of the board of governors. And then he was across the southwestern corner of Connecticut and out over the Sound. Charlie put on the flying helmet and buckled the chin strap. He would give the Mustang a little workout, and he did not want a hard-plastic flying helmet bouncing around the cockpit. He did not bother to plug into the radio jacks. He was free of the Earth for the moment and all its travail. There was time enough to go back to it.

Unbeknownst to Charlie, someone at the airport had pointed out his car and tracked the license plate through the state police. Laura Billings gasped when the call came. She immediately called Jerry.

Charlie marveled at the performance of the Mustang. It was, except for armament, combat ready. It was faster than he remembered it. It handled beautifully. He tried every maneuver he had learned those many years ago. After an hour and a half, he had run through his repertoire twice. He thought about the young man in the red flying suit back at the airport. The poor son of a bitch must be going out of his mind. Well—Charlie had had his fun and more. He had felt something drain out of him, something poisonous. *Pulled* out of him, actually. Out through the pores of his skin by the magnified forces of gravity. He plugged in the radio jacks.

"—calling Mustang! Westchester Tower calling Mustang! Do you read?" he heard. He pressed the mike button on the control stick.

"Mustang to Westchester Tower," he said in a calm voice. "I read you."

"What the devil are you up to?" the voice said.

"I'm over Long Island Sound at five thousand on a heading of one ninety. Instructions." He heard the controller say over the open mike "He's coming in."

"Let down at three hundred feet a minute on your present heading," the controller said. "Are you going to land? Can you land? Do you have experience—" The controller broke off. He came back on after a moment.

"Mr. Billings," the controller said, "your son Gerald is here. He has told us that you were a pilot and have experience in Mustang-type aircraft. He wants to speak to you."

Charlie pressed his lips together. Reality.

"Dad!" Jerry said. "Are you OK? For God's sake, come down! Don't do—do—anything! It will be alright! We love you, Dad. Honest! Please, Dad!" The controller came on.

"Mr. Billings," he said, "you have a very worried family."

"Mustang to tower," Charlie said. "I should be over the airfield in a minute or two. Give me a runway."

"Mustang, we have you in sight," the controller said. "Runway one-fiver. We have cleared all traffic. You are next to land."

Charlie was now at one thousand feet, about two miles from the end of the runway. He could actually make out a crowd of people lining the fence on either side of the terminal. The north end of the airport, where the Air National Guard was tenanted, was also crowded. He could spot the flashing lights atop police, airport security, and state trooper vehicles. Crash trucks waited on either side of the runway at the taxi turnoffs.

"Oh, Christ!" Charlie said to himself, and to the controller, "Mustang on final." He reached for the landing gear switch and cut back on his power. But he did not lower the gear. *This will never happen again,* he thought. He advanced the throttle. The engine roared, and the Mustang accelerated with such force that his head was pushed back against the leather-padded headrest. He had never landed a P-51 without a victory roll over the runway. The last time that had happened was over an airstrip in Germany on V-E Day in 1945.

He dropped the nose of the Mustang a bit until he was just a hundred feet over the runway—give or take. He leveled off. The airspeed indicator read 450 miles per hour. He began his roll as he came even with the Air Guard area. He rolled once. The nose never wavered from level flight. He rolled again and then again until he reached the end of the runway. He came out of his final roll in level flight, pulled back on the stick, and climbed straight up, rolling the aircraft again and again. At seven thousand feet, he stopped the roll.

On the ground, the watchers saw the Mustang reach the top of its ascent. It continued up and over onto its back and then headed straight down. It came down like a bullet and then began to arc out of its dive. The crowd gasped as one and fell silent as the Mustang disappeared behind a hill. There was no sound, no sound at all, it seemed. Jerry Billings, standing with two state troopers, said, "Oh, God!" An airport security guard held up his walkie-talkie, which was tuned to tower frequency.

"Mustang to tower," it crackled suddenly. "On final, coming straight in." Then the Mustang appeared at treetop height. Its gear and flaps were down. It touched the runway almost delicately and rolled a bit. The tail dropped as the plane slowed. It stopped and turned and taxied back up the runway, followed by the crash trucks. A roar went up from the now sizeable crowd.

"Idiots," a security man said.

The Mustang stopped on the grass in front of the service hangar. Everybody waited until the propeller had stopped turning before they moved. Charlie slid back the canopy and got out of the Mustang. He felt exhausted and stiff, but light. He stepped off the wing onto the ground as the first of the crowd, two airport security men, reached him and grabbed him by the arms.

"I'll go quietly!" Charlie said. "You don't have to get tough."

"Shut your goddamn mouth!" one of them said.

A state trooper moved in. "We'll take charge!" he said. "Let him go." The security men released Charlie. Another trooper appeared. The troopers, with the security men clearing the way through the throng, led Charlie to a waiting cruiser. Jerry tried to reach his father, but Charlie was in the car and gone before he was able to. He ran to his own car and followed the state police cruiser.

Charlie was held and questioned for more than an hour at the county police station. He was beginning to regret his adventure.

Maybe he was in more trouble than he thought. The owner of the Mustang was brought in to confront him. If the young pilot felt any anger, it seemed to have spent itself.

"I'm sorry," Charlie said to him. "I'll pay for any damage. I don't think I did any. It's a beautiful airplane. I envy you."

"Your son said you flew them in combat," the young man said.

"Yes," Charlie said.

"I guess that was really something else."

"Yes," Charlie said.

"That was a nice piece of flying," the pilot said.

He said he would send Charlie a bill for the fuel and any damage. He went out then. He seemed almost sorry to go. Someone, probably Laura, had called a friend of the family, who in turn contacted a judge who appeared at the police station. Jerry had come in with the judge, who lectured Charlie as the state trooper had earlier that day. He set a date for Charlie's appearance in court and released Charlie into Jerry's custody. After the judge had ruled and Charlie and Jerry both agreed to the terms, Jerry embraced Charlie. Charlie did not know how he himself felt. He could not know what Jerry felt. He was chastened by being placed in the custody of his son.

They left the police station in silence, the emotion of the moment subdued, if not gone. Walking across the parking lot toward Jerry's Camaro, Charlie spoke first. "How's your mother?" he asked.

"You know," Jerry said, "spastic. I haven't seen her yet. She called me in a panic. Told me I had to get to the airport right away. And that I might have to identify your body. I thought she might be overreacting."

"You don't say," Charlie said.

That would be the next crisis. But it didn't bother him. It would pass. Like all the other minor and major catastrophes. They reached the car. Charlie got in on the passenger side. Jerry got in behind the wheel.

"Your car is still at the airport," Jerry said. "You OK to drive it home?"

"Of course," Charlie said.

Jerry said nothing for a moment. He inserted the key in the ignition but did not start the engine. "Why did you do it, Dad?" he asked.

"You'd have to be an old ex-fighter pilot to understand that, Jerry," Charlie said.

"Are you sorry?"

"Not one goddamn bit," Charlie said. Jerry nodded seriously.

"That make any sense?" Charlie asked him.

Jerry said nothing. Then he began to chuckle. The chuckle erupted into a laugh. Suddenly, Jerry slapped his hand hard on top of the dash.

"Oh, WOW!" he said. "Beautiful! That was—Christalmighty!—fantastic! When you came across that airport!" He looked at Charlie and put his arm around his father's. "Dad—that was fan-god-damn-tastic!" They laughed and cried together for a moment. Jerry disengaged, slammed the door shut on his side, and turned the key in the ignition. The engine started immediately. At the same instant, the car stereo erupted into an explosion of rock music. Charlie winced. Jerry looked at him and reached over and turned off the radio. Charlie, in turn, reached over and turned it back on.

"Just not so loud, Jerry," he said.

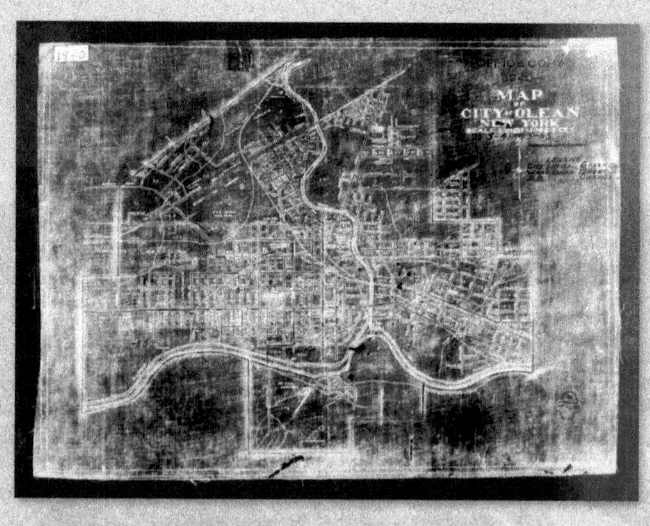
MAP
OF
CITY OF OLEAN
NEW YORK

MR. BIRNBAUM

MR. BIRNBAUM

Harry Birnbaum didn't live in my neighborhood, but he was as well-known as Joe the Cop or Mueller the Butcher. The only thing anybody ever called him was Mr. Birnbaum, and he worked for an insurance company. He went from house to house, apartment to apartment—wherever he had a client—to collect fifty cents for each policy. A policy might be enough for burial or a means of assuring the children of a thousand dollars when they reached twenty-one years of age.

Mr. Birnbaum was tall, stoop-shouldered, and bald. He always wore a gray suit, a white shirt with a dark blue tie, and black shoes with thick gum soles. In the wintertime, he wore a heavy black overcoat with a black muffler and a gray fedora hat. On wet or snowy days, he wore rubbers or galoshes—the black canvas kind with metal clasps—with his trouser cuffs tucked inside. He didn't drive a car but came to the neighborhood by bus at about eight o'clock in the morning, carrying a newspaper and his account book, around which was wrapped a thick rubber band. His clothes always looked too big for him. That and his quiet, soft-spoken manner made him seem to be timid and unhealthy.

Mr. Birnbaum showed up at our house with absolute regularity on Thursdays between three and four o'clock in the afternoon to collect $2.50 from my mother. Mr. Birnbaum would take the money and mark the payment in little squares in his book. My dad's was for burial. Each of us four kids would get a thousand dollars when we reached twenty-one. In times of stress, my mother would say with the sigh of a martyr, "Well—you'll at least be able to bury me."

There were times when my mother didn't have the two-fifty. Mr. Birnbaum would just nod and say, "Next week, then, Mrs. Brady."

Sometimes I would have to go to the door and tell Mr. Birnbaum that my mother wasn't home, and he would say, "Next week, then, William," in that soft voice, and I could never tell if he thought I was telling a lie. There were times when that would happen a couple of weeks in a row. But I never recall Mr. Birnbaum getting upset or demanding payment or threatening to cancel the policies, a prospect that terrified my mother. He always seemed glad to see me and would ask me about school and wish me well before leaving.

Mr. Birnbaum never came inside. He would wait outside in the hall when we lived in the apartment and on the stoop when we moved into the house we rented after my father got a raise. No matter how many times my mother would tell him to come in out of the cold or the heat or whatever, Mr. Birnbaum would apologize and say he didn't want to track up the floor, as if we lived in a mansion instead of an ordinary seven-room frame house on a street with about twenty other houses that—except maybe for a tree or a hedge or a flagpole or some other decoration—looked exactly like ours.

As I said, Mr. Birnbaum was as regular as the days of the week. The milkman was Tuesday. The iceman was usually Friday, and Mr. Birnbaum was Thursday. The only time he ever missed a Thursday was when he was on vacation for two weeks every year. He never told anyone where he spent his vacations. Not that anybody asked him—at least when I was around. But I used to wonder. He would always ask about our family vacations—we would travel to Canada, Washington, D.C., Spring Lake in New Jersey, or a rented bungalow at Rockaway Beach. But he never talked about his own. He would always look tanned and fit, and he stood up straighter, even if he still wore those dumpy-looking clothes. But the tan would fade, and by the middle of October, he looked the way he did the rest of the year.

I graduated from Holy Family Grammar School in 1934 when I was thirteen. I was lucky to win a scholarship to a good Catholic high school in the Bronx, where I would only have to take one bus. One Thursday on our stoop, Mr. Birnbaum congratulated me on the scholarship and gave me a book of poems as a graduation gift. *A Shropshire Lad* by A.E. Housman, an Englishman. It wasn't a new book. In fact, it was very well used. He told me that it was the first book he had ever bought himself when he went to high school in the twenties. I still have it. I had given it to Billy Jr., my only son, a decade before he was killed in Viet Nam. I look at it now and then, and I think about both of them.

I didn't see much of Mr. Birnbaum after I entered high school. I remember that in my second year, he actually came to a play I had a part in, but he didn't stay around afterwards. The play was *The Merchant of Venice*. I played the role of Shylock, of all people, and it wasn't until many years later that I wondered if he had taken any offense. Actually, I would rather that he had come to a football game. I was not an all-star athlete by any means, but I was proud of my athletic letters—I was named twice to the Catholic High School all-star second teams in football and baseball. Mr. Birnbaum knew all this from our conversations. But that visit to my play was the last I saw of Mr. Birnbaum for some time.

The Spanish Civil War broke out that same year. I remember that time particularly because of the effect it had on the neighborhood I lived in. I suppose the same thing happened all over New York and perhaps in other cities with a lot of different nationalities and political factions.

My family and most others in our small part of the Bronx were blue collar, blue uniform and believed that God was a Bronx

Irish Catholic, a Democrat, and a Yankee fan. There were some Protestants and some Jews, too, like Mr. Birnbaum. We had a contented neighborhood. For the most part, it had been spared the economic and spiritual ruin of the Great Depression. People paid little attention to what was happening in Europe. Adolph Hitler and the Nazis were not yet our concern. Not many people worried about what Mussolini was up to in Ethiopia. The talk in our house when "the uncles" came to visit was about jobs and baseball and "that son of a bitch" in the White House. The blue-collar love affair with Franklin Delano Roosevelt had evaporated with his espousal of the political left, especially his recognition of the Russian government—the hated and feared atheistic Communists embodied in Josef Stalin.

But want it or not, the Spanish Civil War divided our community and my family. People took sides mostly without having any considered understanding of what they were taking sides about. For the Catholics, it was as basic as it could be: Franco was a Catholic, and Catholicism was the religion of Spain. The Loyalists were Communists—atheistic Communists!—and they were the archenemy and the Anti-Christ, and whoever supported them was the enemy of the Catholic faith.

I didn't care much one way or the other, although that's not quite right. I had different interests—girls, sports, and learning to drink three or four beers without throwing up. But I couldn't completely escape or pretend that things weren't happening in Europe or at home. Some of my relatives were out of work. My uncle Barney on my mother's side had been a bricklayer. When the Crash came, he went from hundreds of dollars a week to zero. He and his wife, Alice, didn't have any kids, but they were always going to someone's house for a meal or borrowing money "until things change."

It got so tough that Uncle Barney stopped coming around to our house. He was ashamed to be seen in the only suit he had left and the shoes that had been repaired too many times. His shirts, the expensive, custom-made white-on-white shirts of one hundred percent Egyptian cotton, had become frayed at the cuffs and the neck. The cuffs would hang out of the sleeves because he had to sell his gold cufflinks. Aunt Alice got a job as a ticket taker at the Paradise movie theater on the Grand Concourse. She worked from three o'clock in the afternoon until ten o'clock at night, six days a week, and she made maybe twelve dollars. Uncle Barney had to be at the theater to pick her up because there would always be some wiseass who thought he could score with Aunt Alice, who was a very good-looking woman. She was also too friendly, and guys would get the wrong idea. It was always touch-and-go whether Uncle Barney would wind up in a street fight.

The upshot was that one day, Alice took a walk. She left a note and a ten-dollar bill on the kitchen table. That's when Barney joined the Communist Party. He said that it was either that or kill himself. I never did figure that one out. He was not allowed in the house after joining the Party until he swore never to engage in any political arguments.

Uncle Philly on my mother's side was a cop, and he worked out of the West 42nd Street station house in Manhattan, which is now called Midtown North. Uncle Philly was in plainclothes—which was a cop from the uniformed force on detective duty. You can bet that Uncle Philly did alright. He had a house in the Pelham Bay section of the Bronx that didn't cost him a dime to build, to hear my Uncle Mike tell it. Friendly merchants "donated" materials, and other cops donated the labor.

The main reason Uncle Philly did so well was that all the old speakeasies from Prohibition days were in that Manhattan precinct. The best of the survivors became expensive restaurants or jazz joints. Uncle Philly and his partner, who was killed trying to stop an armed robbery, worked all over the precinct, which included the high-priced joints on Fifty-Second Street as well as the gin mills and the flea circuses and the clip joints on Broadway. It also boasted Madison Square Garden on Eighth between Forty-Ninth and Fiftieth, what I would call the Old Garden.

I developed a genuine dislike for my uncle Philly early on. He was a very physical man and liked to push people around. He drank a lot, always beer, in our house. He'd sweat like a bull, and when I or my brother Eddie came in the room, it only meant beer breath, pain, and embarrassment. He'd razz us or give us a shot in the arm and laugh when we flinched. If we were close enough, he'd grab us and put us in a headlock. "Just like I do with the bad guys," he'd say.

Uncle Philly and Uncle Barney rarely agreed on anything. Uncle Philly was a Yankees fan. Uncle Barney rooted for the Giants. But after Uncle Barney became a Communist, he avoided Uncle Philly as much as he could. And on those times when they were together at our house, Uncle Philly would goad Uncle Barney, calling him a Red, hoping he'd take the bait and get tossed out of the house by my father. My father was wise to it, though, and would tell Uncle Philly to knock it off.

In early 1939, the only thing I had in my sights was graduating from high school in June. It was a Monday night in late February, the night of the Rally for America, that interrupted that focus and brought the troubles in Europe to the city and my family.

The rally was held at Madison Square Garden. A group of us from school took the subway from the Bronx to Fiftieth Street and Eighth Avenue because that's what everyone was doing, and it was all Uncle Barney was talking about. He said he was going to protest the Nazis, but I didn't quite believe him.

The Rally, which had been billed as a celebration of America and George Washington's birthday, was anything but. It was a pro-Nazi rally, complete with the national anthem, heil Hitlers, and swastikas on either side of the American Flag. The organizers predicted a sold-out house. The police expected a large crowd of protestors. The rally generated strong opinions. Anger that it was happening in the first place and a fear that the country would get involved in a larger war.

My friends and I came out of the subway into a dense sea of people that stretched for a couple of blocks on Eighth on either side of the Garden. We did our best ducking in and out through the crowd, inching across the avenue.

There was a break in the crowd as we got closer to the Garden. That's when I saw Uncle Philly on duty. He was standing on the corner, looking out at the spectacle in front of him, alert to any flare-ups. I turned away just as the break closed. I don't think he saw me, which was just as well.

Police were everywhere by eight o'clock when the rally started. Cops on horseback formed a wall between the protestors and the entrance to the Garden. A small group of Socialist Workers Party protestors held ground with their signs near the front of the building. Being opposed to both the Nazis and the Communists, my friends and I had our pick of which group we wanted to go after. The larger part of the crowd was there because they hated Nazis, but everyone hated the Socialists.

We saw a few people from the Socialist Workers Party get separated from their larger group. They found themselves in between the police line and the anti-Nazi protestors. I could see that one man wearing a gray wool cap was out ahead of them and being shoved and pushed as he walked. Someone pushed the man into a mounted police officer.

The cop swung his billy club at the man and caught him above the left eye. The blow knocked him down hard. It looked like he was bleeding. He put his hand to his head, and I could see his cap turning red from the blood.

The man stood up, but the press of the crowd pushed him back against the cop. The man reached out his hand, I think to steady himself, and it pressed against the cop's leg. The cop must have thought the guy was trying to pull him off his horse. He jerked his revolver out of its holster. Someone screamed, "No! No!—He's gonna shoot!" Things got crazier then. It was something I'll never forget. The noise was terrifying. I was scared. The cop was, too. I remember being afraid that the cop would shoot and we'd get torn to bits by the demonstrators. We ran back across Eighth Avenue and, from a safe distance, stopped to watch.

The man I saw get hit seemed to have disappeared in the darkness of the evening. But I spotted him again as he crossed the street to the uptown IRT subway entrance. He stopped at the top of the steps, steadying himself against a light post. He wiped his bloodied face with his handkerchief. He removed his bloodstained cap and held it in his hand, then suddenly flung it to the ground as if he was seized by a spasm of rage. He jammed the handkerchief in his pocket and sort of squared himself. The light from the streetlight fell on his face, and I got a good look at him. It was Mr. Birnbaum.

I yelled to him. He turned, saw me, shook his head violently, and disappeared down the subway steps. I started after him, but my friends held me back. We went right home then, just like we promised.

I told my father about seeing Mr. Birnbaum and what had happened.

My father got really angry. His face flushed, and the muscles in his jaws knotted up. "That policeman had no goddamn right to strike him," he said. "I've seen too bloody much of that sort of thing." The anger left him, and he sighed and shook his head sadly. "I'm very sorry for Mr. Birnbaum. He's a decent man."

Later that week, Uncle Philly said that he ran into Uncle Barney in the crowd. Uncle Barney had a load on and was waving a red flag. Uncle Philly said he grabbed Uncle Barney and dragged him into a bar before he got himself killed.

Mr. Birnbaum never came to our house again. In fact, he never showed up in the neighborhood after that. The insurance guy who took his place didn't know him and couldn't tell my parents what became of him. There was a rumor that the insurance company had fired him.

I still managed to graduate from high school that June of 1939. I got a job selling hot dogs and sodas at the New York World's

Fair. It was my first real job. It would be just for the summer because I had already planned to go to college. Once again, I wasn't paying much attention to what was going on in the world. Oh yes, I knew that Hitler was raising hell and that everybody was sure that war would break out in Europe. Nobody that I knew except maybe my uncles thought about Japan's war in China. Then there was the Hitler-Stalin pact, and the only reason I remember that clearly is that Uncle Barney got into a brawl with some of his political cronies. It was so rowdy that the cops were called to break up the fight. Uncle Barney quit the Communists and joined the Democratic Party and got a supervisor's job with the Public Works Administration.

If I wasn't that much concerned about the prospects of war in Europe, my father was. He'd be up late every night, listening to the shortwave broadcasts from Berlin and London and Paris. New York had a dozen or more daily papers, if you counted the different editions. My father would buy six or seven of them, like *The New York Times*, *The Herald Tribune*, *The Sun*, *The Telegram*, *The Post*, *The Journal*, and *The American*. They covered the political spectrum from end to end, and my father read every one of them, trying to fathom the "lunacy"—as he called it—of modern man.

Well, war did come to Europe at the end of that summer, and a year later, as I began my sophomore year at Fordham University, America began drafting men for military service. I was "safe" for the immediate future because of my age. But my older brother Eddie didn't have to wait. He joined the Army Air Corps. My father didn't say much. He knew that sooner or later both my brother and I would be in the service. I would have enlisted myself, but my mother was so upset over Eddie joining up that I decided to wait. My two sisters were too busy being bobby-soxers to worry about anything.

War and anti-war fever broke out all over the place. Some of my classmates went to Canada and volunteered for the Royal Canadian Air Force. Another, Kurt Fliegler, who had been with me in high school, went to join his parents, who had gone back to Germany in 1936 for a "better life." I got a letter from him saying he had been conscripted into the German army. He didn't complain about that. In fact, he was proud of serving "the Fatherland" and predicted a short war and an early victory for Germany. He invited me to visit him when peace came.

In the summer of 1941, my brother got his wings and commission and came home on leave. He had been assigned to a pursuit squadron for combat training. He told us he was sure he would be going to the Philippine Islands. My father was relieved. The Philippines were twelve thousand miles from the European War.

I finally made up my mind that I would not wait for the draft. I went down to the Army Building on Whitehall Street at the tip of Manhattan. I failed the eye test for aviation cadets. I was crushed. An officer told me that I was qualified for Officer Candidate School. I thought about that for a couple of days and went back to the Army Building to sign up. I was told to go home and wait to be called. They were belly deep in OCS candidates without the facilities to train them.

In early October, I got a telegram from the Army, ordering me to report to the Army Building at 0900 hours (it took me a long time to get used to the Army way of telling time and writing dates) on 1 December, which also happened to be my birthday. I'd be twenty years of age, no longer a teenager. That was very important to me.

Eddie sent us a cablegram, telling us he had arrived safely in the Philippines and was anxious to begin flight operations. "Don't worry about the Japs," he told us. "We could whip those monkeys in a week!" We really believed that.

Things got very tense around our house after that. My mother kept my telegram from the Army and the cablegram from Eddie on the sideboard in the dining room. My father followed the progress of the war in Europe and the negotiations in Washington, D.C., in the newspapers and on the radio. He said he was proud of me and my brother for volunteering, but he hoped that we would not have to fight. My father was not a churchgoer. He was not exactly anti-religion, and although he never talked about it to me, I learned that he "lost the faith" on account of "The Troubles" in Ireland. The parish priest in his village in Ireland had refused absolution and the last rites of the church to my father's uncle for political reasons. To the deeply religious "country Irish," such an act was tantamount to condemnation to an eternity in Hell. Yet after the two telegrams arrived, he started to attend Mass—secretly—before starting off to work during the week.

"The war," my mother had said to Father Flynn, who had surprised her when he told her what a joy it was to see my father at the communion rail again.

"Oh," Father Flynn said, "we'll stay out of it. It's not our war, is it? It's Europe's problem. And we should not interfere in Asia. That's none of our business. None whatever."

My mother was not comforted. Father Flynn was young and had been "out of things" while at the seminary. He later died of wounds sustained in Normandy during the Battle for Saint-Lô in 1944.

About 150 other officer candidates were present that Monday morning when I reported at the Army Building on Whitehall Street. The age range for Officer Candidate School was from eighteen to twenty-seven. So, it was a pretty odd assortment of adult and near-adult males who showed up in every assortment of clothing imaginable. They looked like university graduates, professional men, college students, laborers, salesmen, office clerks.

We were all assembled in a fairly large room empty of furniture except for a scarred steel table with a green top. There was a photograph of President Roosevelt on the wall behind the table, with the American flag on one side of it and another flag—probably the War Department flag—on the other side.

An officer and a sergeant organized us by alphabetical order into generally straight rows for a briefing on what we were about to undergo. The fellow right before me said he was a Yale grad. He wore a finely tailored suit, a Chesterfield overcoat, and a pearl gray fedora. He didn't seem the least bit self-conscious. The one after me had just started his junior year at City College. The Yalie asked him if he was Jewish. The answer was, no, he was not. The Yalie simply said "Oh," as if the question had been perfectly proper.

When the mumbling and the shuffling had subsided, the officer read the oath of enlistment "for the duration of the war plus six months." We weren't at war yet, but that didn't seem to matter. When the reading of the oath was finished, the officer told us to signify our acceptance by stepping forward one pace. Those who were unwilling to take the oath—which was final and irrevocable—were to step out and leave the room.

None of us broke ranks. We all took that one step forward.

"Congratulations," the officer said. "You are now privates in the United States Army."

Although we had not been told to bring along any clothing or toilet articles, I had half expected that we would be shipped immediately to some remote Army post to begin training. Instead, we were sent home to wait for orders, assigning us to whatever school the Army decided to send us.

The City College student and I went into a coffee shop for lunch. He was very unsure that he had done the right thing. I was a little doubtful myself. Neither of us had the slightest inkling of what life as a soldier might be like—officer or not. And I don't think he had a clear idea of why he had enlisted any more than I did.

Dinner that evening was a quiet one. My girlfriend, Helen Finnerty, was there. I had told her even before I told my parents of my intention to enlist. She had tried to talk me out of it. We had never talked about marriage, but I think that that's what she had on her mind for when I got out of college.

There was a lot of soft weeping at the table. My mother would tear up and Helen would cry. They'd stop and then Helen would start all over again. By the time dinner was finished, even my kid sisters were crying. My father muttered, "Christ!" and left the table. I followed him into the kitchen.

"What do you think, Pop?" I asked him. "Should I have waited?" He didn't speak for a bit.

"We're going to be at war soon," he said. "A week. A month. Tomorrow. You did what you felt you had to do. I won't question that. If I could go in your place—Eddie's place—I'd do that. If I was called, I'd go. Ah! There's small chance of that." He frowned deeply. I had the feeling that he wanted to say more. Instead, he went to the cupboard and took out two shot glasses. From another, he took a bottle of Irish whisky—a bottle that came out of its hiding place only on the most special occasions.

"Will you take it neat?" he asked. A little stunned by what was happening, I merely nodded. He filled both glasses, corked the bottle, and put it away. Then he handed me one of the glasses.

"Good luck to you, then, Billy," he said. He drained his glass in a gulp, rinsed it, and set it down. I sipped my drink. I could have downed it as he had done. It wasn't as if it was my first drink of strong waters. He watched me. I knew he was not fooled. I didn't have to pretend. I finished my drink and washed the glass as he had done. He left the kitchen. I put the shot glasses back into the cupboard. I felt as if I had received the sacrament of confirmation a second time.

I didn't return to classes. I saw some of my teachers and told them I had enlisted. By now, it had become ritual to them that a student—or even one of their colleagues—would visit them or telephone them or write them with the same news. I've often wished one of them might have said something memorable to me. They were, after all, priests and laymen alike, men of education and wisdom and compassion. But all I got was a handshake, "God go with you!" and "Make us proud of you!"—that sort of thing. I was a private now in Uncle Sam's Army. I certainly didn't feel like a soldier, and still at home and wearing the same clothing I always did, I sure didn't look like one. But something had changed for me. My home was now only a temporary stopping place. My parents and my sisters regarded me differently. Almost as if I had contracted a disease that could not be described or understood. My possessions, school pennants, magazines, skates, odds and ends that kids acquire along the way—treasures once—began to lose their value.

I wanted to talk to someone, but not being on campus and associating with my classmates and teachers, there was nobody. I wasn't afraid. I was anxious, impatient. Talking about what I was about to do would help. For the first time in a couple of years, I thought about Mr. Birnbaum. He would be the kind of guy I could talk to. He had always listened. But he was gone to wherever those people who populate one's childhood disappear to. I found myself picking up the poetry book he had given me, *A Shropshire Lad*. I'd never read much of it before. I hadn't been willing to read about dying.

My call from the Army came nine days later—three days after Pearl Harbor. My mother was already in a state of shock over the attack and the news that the Japs had also attacked the Philippines. Frankly, I was relieved to get the call.

My leave-taking was an emotional one. I refused to have my parents or even Helen Finnerty come downtown to the Whitehall Building to see me off. I took only a small bag with some toilet articles, a couple of changes of underwear, extra socks, and a clean shirt. I wore a windbreaker and sweater over a shirt and trousers. It was cold and windy, but I felt a hat would be too much of a problem. I took the D train on the first leg of a journey that would cover four years and thousands of miles, a half dozen of these United States, and a couple of continents.

Before I left for the Army, my Uncle Philly had given me the only piece of advice that was worth anything. Naturally, he stressed his point with a whack on the arm.

"Billy," he said, "you can't beat the system. So don't try. Roll with the punches." (Whack!) "Y'know what I mean?"

There were no punches in basic training, of course. A lot of threats. A lot of shouting and a lot of marble-mouth Southern jargon. I survived it all and came out of OCS a second lieutenant of the infantry. Better known as the Queen of Battle. I heard that a lot and wasn't quite sure what it meant. I would find out soon enough.

Halfway through OCS, I got a letter from my mother telling me that Eddie was safe. He had been ordered to China to join a new pursuit squadron that was being formed around the Flying Tigers, the American volunteer group of pilots who fought the Japanese under Chennault. The only other really unexpected thing that happened before I finished OCS was a letter I got from Captain Harry Birnbaum, USA. He was in the Army! He said he had read about my enlistment in *The Bronx Home News*, which was sent to him by his wife. He wished me luck and hoped that our paths would cross again. The letter had been sent to my home, and my parents had forwarded it. It bore an Army Post Office franking, which meant that Mister—Captain—Birnbaum was overseas.

The next couple of years were not atypical for a new lieutenant. There was a lot of training. There was a lot of helling around. I matured quickly—if that's the word. I got a letter from Helen Finnerty. Right. A "Dear John" letter. I wasn't upset. I wasn't elated. That world was growing further and further away.

My first taste of battle was North Africa in 1943. I was a replacement as a platoon leader with an outfit that had been mauled at Kasserine, the Army's first encounter with the Nazis. I reported a week after I got off the troop ship at Casablanca. A clutch of unbloodied second lieutenants was hurried into the line with the shine still on their shoes. Luckily, the front had quieted down, and there was little fighting. But the detritus of battle was all about: tanks, trucks, jeeps all along the roads, blasted and twisted into grotesque shapes as if sculpted by an avant-garde lunatic. American soldiers who were surely as young as I—what was left of them—lay row on row along the roadside, encased in rubber-lined canvas shrouds. The graves registration teams were out searching for the MIAs—those unaccounted for in the aftermath of battle. There were rotting carcasses of dead animals and dead innocents—the locals who had come to watch the fighting, believing, I supposed, that it would not envelop them. I learned later that many of those dead had simply been waiting for the battle to move along so that they might rush in to strip the soldiers dead—American and German alike—of whatever had even the slightest value. And not all those innocents had been killed during the battle but rather afterward as looters and ghouls. There were ambulatory wounded, waiting in clusters for the trucks that would transport them back to a general hospital well away from here. Only a fool would not pause to reflect that he was staring at the savage face of war. I could never again, I was sure, experience the same sense of shock as those first encounters with death and ruin. I was wrong. It would only get worse.

After North Africa came Sicily, then Salerno and Anzio, where I took a bullet in my arm and made first lieutenant. My wound was serious but not serious enough for a trip back to the States. When I got out of the hospital in Anzio, I went to Rome, which by that time had been abandoned by the Germans. I went to Mass at St. Peter's, saw the Pope, and toured the Vatican. Then I pursued other interests less lofty than sightseeing in Vatican City. Rome was my carnival for three crazy days. My mother wanted to know if I had learned any Italian. My father had a heart attack and had to retire. The war kept me from worrying about him.

We'd been hearing about an invasion of Western Europe for months. Then it came, and I said a fervent prayer of thanks that I had missed it. I hated beach assaults. Then about a month afterward, our outfit was pulled out of the line at Anzio. We were going to hit the south coast of France to create a second front to force the Germans to fight a rearguard action and take the pressure off the invasion forces.

The landing in France was not exactly a piece of cake, but it went a lot better than Anzio—or Normandy. We were going, as Patton said, like shit through a goose.

I got my second wound in the Colmar Pocket in eastern France, not far from the German border. It was the kind of wound that could have killed me. How it didn't, even the surgeons couldn't say. My guts were torn up from mortar fragments, and I lost a lot of blood before I was brought to a field station. I wound up in a general hospital in England. It took me three months to recover enough to get around on my own. By that time, the Battle of the Bulge was raging, and there was talk of sending any ambulatory patients, even if not fully recovered, back to the Continent.

I wasn't too sure whether I wanted to go back to the States or rejoin my division in France. The Army made the decision for me. I went back to the division. I was just as glad. I decided I wanted to be in at the finish. The German attack had stalled. It was only a matter of time now.

Getting back to my company was ten times worse than trying to get from the Bronx to the Jersey shore on a Friday in August. I hopped a ride in a C-47 from England to France. I hitched rides in everything from a jeep to a half-track. There were thousands of German prisoners sitting alongside the roads in huge clusters. I saw one group of almost battalion size sitting in a field, with one G.I. with an M1 guarding them. They wanted no more war. You didn't have to be very bright to see that. Then there were the refugees, the slave laborers, and God knows what else. They wanted food and water and medical help, and the U.S. Army did its best.

I passed one concentration camp, Dachau. It was fairly empty, but there were still skeletons with a layer of skin shuffling around, hollow-eyed and gape-mouthed. The German people we saw were hostile and scared. That made me feel as good as you can in the middle of all the chaos and destruction they had caused. I felt sorry for the German children, especially one five- or six-year-old boy with his right hand missing. But then I thought of the little village of Oradour-sur-Glane I had seen back in France, where an SS Panzer division had locked up a couple of hundred men, women, and children in the village church and set fire to it. It was in reprisal for the killing of an SS officer—one single officer—by the Resistance. That memory tempered any feelings of sympathy I felt, even for a maimed child.

Civilians from the villages around the concentration camp had been conscripted to help bury the dead and take care of the still living who hadn't been evacuated yet. We smelled the stench of the place before we actually saw the ugly stone-and-brick main entrance. I had expected to see barbed wire fences with gates. But this looked exactly like a prison.

We got a tour of the place. It's still something I hate to recall. I'll just say that I finally felt a lightning bolt of understanding of just why the war was necessary. I vowed that when I got home, I would batter my uncles with what I'd seen. They all believed that the noblest thing a man—a real man—could do was to go to war. But none of them had ever been to war.

We pushed on past Munich into Austria, where there was not a whole lot of real fighting. The company commander's jeep hit a road mine. His driver was killed and the commander was badly injured. I learned later that he had lost a leg and a hand. The irony of it was that the German surrender came little more than a week after Captain Freel was injured. No matter how you tried to avoid it, somebody always brought up the possibility that the last guy to die in the European war might be one of us.

I was named acting company commander, and two days later my promotion to captain came down. I wasn't sure how I felt about that. I was twenty-three years old. I didn't want to be the one responsible for getting people killed this close to the end of the war.

I needn't have worried. We got orders to hold our position. Then my insides went haywire and I was evacuated to a general hospital near Munich. That's where I was when the war ended, and that's where I came face-to-face again with Mr. Birnbaum. I was sitting in a day room in my pajamas and bathrobe feeling sorry for myself when he came in. I didn't recognize him at first. He looked taller, and he was a lot thinner. He wore a thin mustache, and the ring of hair around the back and sides of his head was clipped short. He looked hard and tough and tired. He was wearing pressed combat fatigues, boots and all. They looked like they had seen a lot of wear, but they were spit-shined. He wore a Third Army patch on his left shoulder, which meant Patton. That explained why he looked parade-ground sharp.

"I'm looking for Captain William Brady," he said. His voice was the voice of someone who was in charge and knew it.

"Here, sir," I said, and raised my hand. I started to get up from my wheelchair.

"Stay there," he said. He stood in front of me. It must have dawned on him that I hadn't recognized him. He smiled. The second he said "Mr. Birnbaum," I knew him. We shook hands, and even that was different. It was firm. Controlled. He pulled over a chair and sat down.

We chatted about the war. He was a lieutenant colonel and a member of the Military Government group in Munich. His job was war crimes officer. He had been an artillery officer with Patton's Third Army. The secret of how he used to spend his vacations was finally revealed. He had joined the New York National Guard in the early thirties, mostly for the little extra money it paid. When he graduated from college, he got his commission. That was just about the time Hitler became "Der Fuehrer." He told me he had family in Germany at the time and that his parents got letters warning that there would be war.

He leaned toward me and pointed to a scar over his left eyebrow. It was about an inch long and looked very much like the fist tracks you see on a boxer. "Remember that?" he said.

"Yes," I told him. I felt a sting of shame for having been a part of that "pageant" the night he got hit outside the Garden.

"You know," he said, "I was afraid after that to go back to work on my old route. I was sure my picture would be in the paper, and let's face it, a lot—most—of my clients were solid, upstanding patriotic Americans. So, I quit the job and enlisted in the regular army. I was sent to Panama. Coast artillery. At least it was warm.

And sunny. It wasn't much fun, though. I was the only Jew in the battery." He smiled. "I was treated well enough. No insults. No tricks. I was an oddity—a freak. I don't think any of those Southern boys—they were all country boys from the South—had ever even met a Jew before. You know how I spent my free time? A lot of it? I taught some of those Southern boys to read. Really. I enjoyed that." He fell silent, smiling at the recollection.

"I came here to learn about you," he said. "Not to tell you about me." I filled him in on my letters from the family and what I knew of the neighborhood. He asked me about my wounds. I was being treated well, I told him, and would be sent back to the States as soon as a flight was available to England. I'd go the rest of the way by ship.

"Have you been to Dachau?" he asked. The question was casual, as if he were asking if I had seen the latest movie.

"Yes, sir," I said.

"How did you feel about it?" he asked.

"Sick and angry," I said, "and ashamed." His eyebrows went up.

"Ashamed?" he said. "Why would you feel ashamed?"

"I honestly don't know," I told him. "Maybe because it took me so long to understand. And I'm not sure that I do understand even now."

"That perhaps will come," he said. "I'm not sure I understand either. The war here is finished. I should be elated. We stopped the Nazis. We smashed the Hun—again. We won. Right? I wonder. They had me investigating war crimes—atrocities. I could live to be a hundred more years, and I would never be finished. If there is a hell, that would be it for me. An eternity of—of—pornography, Bill"—I was surprised at that—"the human spirit can tolerate only so much hate. It can't grow any more intense. A numbness sets in. I've visited all of the concentration camps we and the British have liberated. I've interviewed hundreds and hundreds of survivors. Jews, Christians, atheists, writers, educators, policemen, children, shopkeepers—shopkeepers! Imagine! And I can't get any angrier.

I think if I don't get the hell out of this, I'll lose my mind."

He stood abruptly and stuck out his hand. "See you back home, Captain," he said. "Keep your head up and your ass down, soldier." We shook hands, and he turned and left.

I did move out a week later. They kept me in England for another month, and I finally sailed back to New York aboard the Queen Mary. I carved my initials on the rail of the promenade deck like so many other G.I.s. My parents and sisters were at the pier in Hoboken. Our reunion was marred by the news that my brother was missing in action. I was sent to St. Albans Hospital on Staten Island for surgery on my gut, which was successful. By the time I was declared fit to return to duty, Japan had surrendered. Eddie turned up in a Japanese prisoner-of-war camp pretty much the worse for wear.

Both Eddie and I had some trouble readjusting to civilian life. Eddie went back into the Army Air Force. I finished college and went to work, like my father, for the telephone company. I got married and the kids came along and the promotions came. We moved to Westchester County, where we, my wife and I, still live. My father passed away one year after he retired. My mother died many years later at the age of eighty-eight. They're both buried in Gate of Heaven Cemetery.

I really have no complaints about my life. I survived the war. I prospered. My health has been good despite everything. Eddie retired from the Air Force a full colonel and lives in Texas. No kids, but a lot of golf and fishing. My wife and I are grandparents five times over. Our daughters enjoy solid marriages. My sisters, both married with kids, live out of state. We get together at least once a year. Now that I've retired, my wife and I travel as much as we can and drop in on family whenever we can. I don't belong to any veterans' organizations. I play golf at least once a week with a couple of good friends who happen to be combat veterans. But we stopped talking about "The War" a long time ago. One of the guys goes to his division reunion. He always comes back depressed.

What I miss most of all is my son Billy. He was a good kid. A fine athlete. He still had some corners to be knocked off, so he joined the Air Force out of college and became a pilot. He was one of the early birds in Viet Nam. He went because it was his job. He used to write that he didn't understand what the hell we were doing there. But he stuck it out. Coming back from a mission to his air base at Da Nang, he took ground fire from "Charlie" in the hills and ran into the side of a mountain.

Pinelawn is a national cemetery two-thirds of the way out on Long Island. Billy is buried there. I go out to visit him whenever the weather is good. I used to go more often, but it's a long drive out and back by myself. My wife isn't that well. Not sick, really, but not all that well either. I make sure that one of the days I drive out to Pinelawn is Memorial Day. No matter what. I've not missed one since he came home.

This year I thought I would have to pass it up because my car was on the blink. The dealer soaked me, but the car got fixed. The weather was perfect. Mild. A few clouds. A light breeze. I welcomed the walk from the parking area to the gravesite. Billy's headstone was, like all the others, simple.

1ST LT. WILLIAM T. BRADY, JR. USAF—KIA JUNE 27, 1968—DA NANG, SOUTH VIET NAM

I stood for a couple of minutes and, as I always do, began to walk among the headstones, sort of visiting. I'd say a little prayer—silently, of course. Just "Rest in peace." That's all. Then I'd go back to Billy's grave, touch the top of the headstone, and leave.

I had walked a little farther than usual and found myself near the chapel and the "Wall of Honor," on which were inscribed the names of those whose remains have never been recovered because "they lie in unknown graves." There was a familiar figure standing at the wall. Even from the back, I knew it was Mr. Birnbaum. The old stoop was there, and his overcoat seemed too large for him. I went over and stood next to him. He turned and said, "Hello, Billy. I saw you awhile back. I wondered if that William Brady was related to you."

"My son," I said.

He pointed to the wall. "Mine's up there," he said. I scanned the row of names he was pointing at and saw 1ST LT. HERBERT BIRNBAUM, USMC—MIA JANUARY 6, 1971—SOUTH VIET NAM.

"I'm sorry," I said.

"Yes," he said. "So am I—for both of us."

Neither one of us said anything for a few moments.

"Do you understand it all yet?" he asked.

"No," I said. "I've stopped trying. As the song says, 'Your life is what happens to you.'"

"War," Mr. Birnbaum said. "What a useless occupation."

We parted then. Oh yes, we exchanged cards. He had retired—from what I had not asked—and lived with his wife in Boca Raton, Florida. I promised to visit if I ever got down that way. Walking back to Billy's grave, I thought how neither I nor Mr. Birnbaum had told the other how our sons died. I suppose it really made no difference in the long run. I patted the top of Billy's headstone and said a silent "Rest in peace." The last I saw of Mr. Birnbaum, he was driving his car toward the gate. He saw me and waved. I waved back. I don't think he saw it, but I know he knew I had waved back. He might have smiled. My wave was more of a salute. Well—why not? It's a soldier's way.

Driving home from Pinelawn has always been very difficult for me. It was especially so that day as I tried not to think about all that might have been.

THE UNDEFEATED ROUGH AND TUMBLE CHAMPION OF KANSAS

THE UNDEFEATED ROUGH AND TUMBLE CHAMPION OF KANSAS

I seen this story the other night on the television about this dude who holed himself up in his apartment with a shotgun and various other assorted lethal weaponry, including a gallon of muscatel and some dope his girlfriend said he'd been smoking all night with the wine and some rum before he broke out the firearms and started shooting out streetlights.

About a million cops showed up, it looked like to me on the tube, and Jesus! was it noisy. And there was maybe *two* million rubberneckers out to watch the fun, which was to see the poor sucker get blown away. Well—with all them cops, they could of taken the guy out with no sweat, but they had this special unit which they actually talked that poor crazy nut into walking out of that apartment with his hands on top of his head. It took something like fourteen hours to do, which when you think about it in a city like New York, which is where this thing happened, is a lot of time for an army of cops to waste on one screwball when there's so many running around perpetrating their perpetrations.

When they took the guy out on the street to a patrol car, I seen this one cop give the guy a cigarette. The guy was about thirty, thirty-five, and wore this beard and a checkered shirt and jeans and no shoes and he was crying and the cops—you could see it even on television—looked like they was sorry for him. And when they showed the crowd, you seen kids grinning and making waggle-ears at the camera and the older people with beer bellies and some with curlers in their hair looking mad and shaking their fists at the guy. His girlfriend was there too, and she had long stringy hair and could of been pretty except for a wiped-out look on her face. The cops wouldn't let her get in the car with her boyfriend and some news guy stuck a mike at her mouth so quick, she had to back away or she might of got a couple of teeth knocked out. And I read in the paper the next day that the boyfriend was a Viet Nam veteran and couldn't hold a job or anything and was strung out on dope and booze. Well—that Viet Nam thing was so long ago he should of gotten himself all straightened away by this time. At least that was the way it looked like to me that people was thinking, and that the best thing they could of done for that poor bastard was to lock him up in a rubber room and weld the door shut. And I got mad at that. I mean, what did they know about what was going on inside that poor guy's head? I don't just mean the Viet Nam thing. I mean that maybe was his monkey. And the monkey turned into a gorilla and before you know it—ZAP!

I got to thinking about that whole thing and how people really didn't give one goddamn about what was bugging the guy. You couldn't hear the words but you just knew they was calling him some pretty bad names or they was laughing at him. *Laughing*! Except the cops. They felt sorry for him. Them and his girlfriend. And I got to remembering a thing like that that happened a long time ago when I happened to be in Kansas.

It ain't really a part of the story but I was in a combat engineers regiment attached to the First Army in World War II. Before that I was a kid in the Bronx learning how to drink five beers in a row without throwing up, and the Army took me and taught me a trade. It wasn't no June Walk, that war. I mean, I seen a lot of action from D-Day plus One right on up to the end, and I can tell you things got very hairy once in a while. But I got through it o.k. and I didn't come home with any hang-ups that I can remember. Well—I got into the Ironworkers Union and got married. Win one, lose one. But the marriage didn't work out and that's how come I happened to be in Kansas. You see, I got *two* families mad at me. Hers and mine. They didn't believe in divorce and my wife had four brothers and three of them was ex-Marines and the other was an ex-swabbie and they was Irish like me and we came from the South Bronx, the old South Bronx, and I would of had to fight them four wild men six days a week one at a time. Now, I could handle myself pretty good in them days and maybe I could of took on two of them in a row. But four of them! I'd of had a better chance against a subway train. So I packed my coveralls, burner's gloves, steel-toed work shoes, and my union book and took a walk.

There was a lot of work around the country in those days and I could pick and choose. I could send a few bucks a week to my ex to keep her from sending the cops after me and still have a bundle left over. I was doing a lot of drinking, but I was young and strong and didn't have no trouble on any job I had. I could spend the night boozing it up in some bucket of blood and still be on the job on time and ready to work. It wasn't no big thing to walk a six-inch I-beam a hundred and sixty feet in the air. I never dropped a wrench or fell or caught a hot rivet in my pants. But when the whistle blew I went looking for the action. And I usually found it.

It was around the middle of July in 1949 that I walked off a job in St. Louis where I'd been a few months. The foreman of the gang I was in was an old-timer and he didn't like young snots like me who was a rated journeyman ironworker at twenty-five, especially a New Yorker. He went on and on about how he was a helper for eight years before he got to be a journeyman when the war started, and I got so sick of hearing that I told him maybe he was just stupid, and he tried to belt me with a spud-wrench, but he missed and I decked him. Well, he got me arrested and the local Justice of the Peace fined me the exact amount of pay I had coming, so I headed west with maybe forty bucks in my jeans, which would not buy me a ticket to anyplace important. I put my union button on the front of this wool cap I always wore and my "ruptured duck," a little gold-colored button they gave you to wear after you are discharged so people would know you did your bit and wasn't holding two defense jobs and making a bundle while guys like me was out there dying and getting drunk and laid in foreign climes. I went down to the docks to where all the over-the-road rigs came and asked around for a lift going west, and this trucker, nice guy, Hank, a family man with his own tractor who was with the Second Armored Division, I think, took me along. "Well, I'm only going as far as Wichita, Kansas," he said, "but you wouldn't have no trouble there picking up a ride for California or San Francisco if that's where yer heading." I told him I had no place special in mind, and I was looking for work, and he told me that there was some construction going on at the Boeing plant outside Wichita and maybe I could hook on there.

We took off from St. Louis about four in the morning and I wasn't a bit sorry to kick the dust of that town from my feet, as the Bible says. I had this bottle of Old Grand-Dad and I took it out and offered Hank a drink.

"Put that thing away or get out of the cab," he told me. "I'm Mormon. Me and the jug are mortal enemies," he says. Not nasty. More like my Uncle Terence who was born in Ireland and was a "Pioneer," which was a society which you joined when you were a little kid and swore that you would never taste alcohol under pain of mortal sin and like that. "You would be better off if you took and threw that thing out the window," my friend said. "But far enough so it don't land on the road and shatter and maybe some unfortunate behind us wouldn't roll over the pieces of broken glass and get a blowout and get killed." And that's the way Hank talked. And he could quote sayings from the Bible the way I could tell dirty jokes without thinking hard. I think I said only one bad word on that trip, which lasted about eleven hours including stops, and I didn't tell a single dirty joke.

The minute I was in Kansas, I knew I wasn't going to like the place, although I didn't tell my friend that. I mean, *flat*. There wasn't so much as a bump or dip it seems like now. All I seen was corn, corn, and dinky towns that looked like they were bought out of a used town catalog. That was thirty-odd years ago and maybe Kansas has changed, but I doubt it. There's no way you're going to change that flatness without an earthquake or something. I mean, New York has hills and streets that go every which way, and you don't have to go a couple of hundred miles before you see something different. And the Kansas people talked the same way—flat. They're o.k. as far as people go, I guess. But I didn't meet a hell of a lot of Kansas people while I was there anyway, which I'll explain.

My Mormon friend dropped me off a little outside Wichita in front of a beat-up looking clapboard house that he said took in roomers. It was run by a guy and his wife that came from "back east in Missouri," which made me smile. I paid them fifteen dollars for the week, which wasn't bad since I got two meals. Right away I hitched a ride to the Boeing plant, which was maybe another ten miles down the road. Now, this is what I mean about not meeting a whole lot of people from Kansas. It looked like everybody who worked at Boeing came from some-place else, Texas and Arkansas and Oklahoma and Montana and places like that. I didn't meet one New Yorker. Anyway, they was still using rivets in those days and I was a riveter among other things, so they took me on just like Hank said, and I went to work the next morning.

Like I said before, when I wasn't working I went looking for where the action was, and I figured I would have one hell of a long look finding anything in Wichita. I mean, they had this liquor law where you couldn't buy drinks in a restaurant. You had to buy a bottle and sneak it into the place and order ginger ale or Squirt or root beer even to mix your drink if you liked it that way. But I wasn't no bottle drinker. I liked my whiskey in a shot glass sitting alongside of my beer, which I also liked to drink out of a glass instead of a bottle. But you got to adapt, so I went along and took my belt out of the bottle wrapped in a brown paper bag and sucked my beer out of a bottle so small they would have got wrecked if they tried to give a guy that in a Bronx gin mill and charge him forty cents for.

But that was the way it was and the places where you could drink like that weren't nothing to write home about. They were usually stuck out in the middle of nowhere, one-story concrete block joints with flat roofs and a big "Blue Ribbon" sign. And the only music was this hillbilly stuff that I didn't like one goddamn bit. But there was this one place that was a little different from the rest. It had a waterfall painted on the side with lights from the roof overhang that lit it up at night and it was called "The Cascades." Somebody told me it used to be an Army building during the war, which I could believe, they all looked like Army buildings. One thing different about The Cascades was that it actually had a little bar, and you could rent a shot glass and a beer glass for a nickel apiece and could drink like a gentleman. They had a jukebox that had things on it like Glenn Miller and Artie Shaw and Stan Kenton besides the hillbilly junk. And on Friday and Saturday nights they had "live entertainment," which I will get to in a minute. First, I got to tell about Cowboy Swensen, which he is the whole point of this story. And before that, Rubberhose.

I worked five and a half days on that Boeing job and got paid on Saturday when we knocked off. I got pretty friendly with a burner they called Rubberhose. He was about six feet eight and skinny as hell. But he was the best burner—that's a guy who uses the oxy-acetylene torch for cutting steel and welding—I ever worked with before or since. He was about forty-five and was a Seabee in the war in the Pacific. He had these false teeth that you could see for a mile and he always wore an old cloth cap even indoors. He liked his booze, a hundred proof bourbon was what he drank.

Maybe that was because he came from Kentucky, where he still had a wife and five or six kids. He told me about The Cascades and said to go there with him if I liked action. They had a stripper there and an acrobatic dancer who looked like a Shetland pony, he said. And maybe I'd get to see Cowboy Swensen in action. I thought maybe he was talking about something dirty and told Rubberhose I didn't go for that kind of thing. I saw one of those type of shows once in Tijuana, Mexico, and I had to go to confession, which I didn't make a habit of usually. And I took two showers a day after that for eight straight days.

But Rubberhose says that it's nothing like that. Cowboy Swensen, he tells me, is a very tough son of a bitch who never lost a rough-and-tumble fight in his life, and the chances were pretty good that, with all the construction workers around, some guy who thought he could take Cowboy would stir Cowboy up.

"You're from back East," Rubberhose tells me on a Saturday night at The Cascades. "But if you was from anywheres between the Mississippi and the Rocky Mountains, especially from Kansas on south, you would of knew about Cowboy Swensen. In the old days he would of been a gunfighter and there would be all these guys trying to knock off Cowboy Swensen and get a reputation." That's how Cowboy Swensen came to own The Cascades.

Rubberhose had got to know Cowboy at an oilfield in Oklahoma where Cowboy was a roughneck and Rubberhose worked on building those drilling rigs. "I just knew him," Rubberhose said. "I wasn't no friend of his. Nobody was. He wasn't mean and wasn't no drinker. He still ain't—a drinker, I mean. He just loved fightin'. Anybody. Anytime. And that's why he had so many jobs. When the war came everybody figured that Cowboy would get his fill of fightin', but he was about thirty-three back in 1941 and he was deaf in one ear from getting hit on it so many times and he had a bad eye where somebody hit him with a wrench, and he couldn't open his right hand full he broke it so many times. So they made him a 4-F and he stayed on in the oil fields." Anyway,

Rubberhose went into the Seabees and didn't hear nothing about Cowboy until after the war. "By that time Cowboy couldn't get a job in the oil fields," he said. "He almost killed the guy down at Ponca City and everybody was a-scared of him. Somebody tried to make a professional boxer out of him but he just wouldn't obey the rules, and that finished that. Then he tried to be a wrestler but he always played for real and he couldn't get no matches, and when I came across him in '45 he was a bouncer in a roadhouse down near Coffeyville.

"He liked that job," Rubberhose said. "It was indoors and he never had to worry about getting fired. He brought the business in with the guys coming from all over to see if they could put Cowboy down in a fight. The place used to get wrecked pretty regular until the guy that owned it got Cowboy to do his fighting outside. And this gave a lot of people a chance to bet, and the owner held all the bets. And Cowboy always bet on himself and made a lot of money until two guys he beat in the same night burned the place down and Cowboy had to go looking for a new job."

Rubberhose took a minute to watch the awful floor show in front of us with a six-foot stripper who had a scar on her belly and didn't go all the way anyhow. And the acrobatic dancer, who did look like a Shetland pony, she was about four feet nothin' and had long blondish kind of hair that came over her eyes and she couldn't dance worth a shit. "Cowboy was getting on by then, about forty I guess, and times was changing," Rubberhose went on.

"The war changed a lot of things, a lot of guys had all the fighting they wanted," Rubberhose said. "They was getting married and raising kids and buying houses, and the only ones who were causing trouble were drunks and guys like Cowboy from the old days. And the towns were getting tougher on that kind of thing anyway. The cops could take care of anything and nothing got busted up."

But there were still a couple of places like The Cascades, for instance. It was outside the Wichita line and the only cops around were the state police and they didn't want nothing to do with the place unless somebody pulled a gun. Which was frequent enough, I guess, since two guys got killed there once.

"Anyways, Cowboy comes up to see about bein' a bouncer here at The Cascades. Fred Poyning who owned the place says he's got a bouncer and Cowboy says could he have the job if he licks the guy. Fred says no at first but then gets to thinking about it. See, this bouncer he had was young and come out of an armored division and was division heavyweight boxing champ. So Fred sees a way to make a lot of money and agrees to Cowboy fighting his guy. But he tells Cowboy, it's got to be out in the parking lot and it's got to be a no-holds-barred fight to the finish, which is o.k. with Cowboy. And Fred is so goddamn sure his boy will take Cowboy that he tells Cowboy that if he wins he gets The Cascades, never mind the job.

"Jesus! You woulda thought it was Joe Louis fighting Jack Dempsey! There musta been a thousand people trying to get in here that night. They come from all over. Fred had to hire a couple of town cops to kinda keep the crowd from getting out of hand. But he was selling bootleg booze by the gallon. I come down from Hutchinson where I was working, and I got to say that that was one fight that will be talked about for a long time. It went on for almost two hours. Cowboy looked like he'd been worked over with an axe. But the other guy looked like he got blowed up. After they took the guy away in the ambulance, Cowboy goes over to Fred and demands a piece of paper giving him The Cascades and Fred says he didn't really mean what he said. But Cowboy acts like he don't hear Fred. He grabs Fred by the arm and pulls him into The Cascades. Now, I can't tell what went on inside that place. But after about ten minutes, Fred come out, gets in his car with his girlfriend and drives away. And nobody ever seen him since."

Well, that was a nice story that Rubberhose told me, and I thought maybe it's true and maybe it ain't. All I know is while we're sitting there Cowboy himself come in and took up behind his bar. He looked to me like a nice mild-mannered guy with a half-bald head and a big belly. He had a flat nose and his eyebrows were all scarred up and there were creases in his face that nature didn't put there. And I saw what Rubberhose meant about his right hand. But my old man had bad arthritis and his hands looked like that. So I figured that maybe Rubberhose was handing me a line because I was from New York City.

In fact, The Cascades was pretty mild compared to some of the places I drank in, and I didn't see a single fight for nearly a month of Friday and Saturday nights. But all Rubberhose would say was "You'll see."

Well, I didn't see, and the Boeing job was winding up and I was getting restless to move on. I was sending money back to my ex and was saving some, which shows you how tame things were in Wichita. And being married once, I didn't feel like no bachelor or guy who wasn't ever, and I was getting kind of lonesome for female company. I met some ladies there in Kansas, especially one who had this beautiful black hair and light blue eyes and was built pretty good. But she didn't talk much and she didn't like sitting with Rubberhose and me and the other guys. I tried but didn't get nowheres with her. So that was a disappointment. So I tried to get something going with the acrobatic dancer and found out she was a Hungarian who married a G.I. and divorced him when she got to the United States and didn't speak hardly any English. And all this time Cowboy Swensen stood behind that little bar watching things with a funny little smile on his face and not talking much. And somehow I began to get the feeling that Rubberhose knew what he was talking about.

The Boeing job finished up on a Friday and I had to hang around until Saturday to get paid off. I worked a lot of overtime that week and had a pretty good paycheck coming. I had half made up my mind to go back to the Bronx and try to pick things up with my ex. I was pretty sure things could be worked out. It wasn't no fun anymore batting around the country just working to eat and go out and get drunk on weekends. And all that flatness in Kansas was getting to me. The other half of my mind was thinking about California, which I never seen, and I was thinking that maybe I would settle down out there and ask my ex to come out there with the kids for a new start. That's right, kids. I forgot to tell you me and my ex had two boys and a girl during the brief time we were man and wife. But I knew I wouldn't make up my whole mind until Saturday after I got paid and checked out of the boardinghouse and went into Wichita to the bus depot to buy a ticket.

Rubberhose was going back to Kentucky, there was a new job starting on a bridge that would go a couple of years, and Rubberhose tried to get me to go with him. But I said it would be either New York or California.

So him and me decided to have one last celebration Saturday night in The Cascades. I wasn't even thinking about Cowboy Swensen anymore.

Nothing went right that day. I got back to the rooming house after work and there was a letter from my ex telling me she got married to a fireman and I didn't have to send no more money. The guy she married was a guy from the neighborhood who wasn't in the service during the war. He was a fireman the whole time and lived with his mother and was forty years old. Well, I couldn't wish them any bad luck. I took the letter up and threw it down the toilet.

When Rubberhose and me got to The Cascades, the stripper and the acrobatic dancer were gone and there was a hillbilly band on the stage. If I'd of known that I would of gone someplace else. But Rubberhose didn't mind. He liked hillbilly music and kept stomping one of his big feet and drinking that hundred proof bourbon.

The place was crowded like I never seen it before. Rubberhose and me sat at the bar at first. Cowboy's girlfriend was working behind the bar, she was a fat lady with a lot of blonde hair and little eyes and a little mouth. She wore these shoes with thick soles and high heels, and she had a lot of trouble walking and I thought she was going to fall down any minute. And she looked scared. She kept looking toward the back door and you'd have to ask her twice for something.

Cowboy came in around ten o'clock and he didn't have that smile on his face.

"Change your shoes and go wait on tables," he told his girlfriend. She didn't argue. When she went, Cowboy put his foot up on the sink behind the bar and leaned his elbows on the bar and started looking around the room. He never moved his head. Just his eyes. There was some college-type kids at a table and one of them came up and asked for four bottles of beer. Cowboy didn't stir. He just looked at the kid.

"You go back to your table and tell the waitress to bring 'em," Cowboy said. "That's what we got waitresses for."

"I've been waiting for ten minutes!" the kid said.

"Go back to your table or I'll peel your head like a goddam onion!" Cowboy said. The kid looked surprised and woulda said something except that a guy sitting at the bar poked him and nodded like he was warning him to go and sit down, and he did.

Rubberhose nudged me. He had his glass in his hand. "I'm going to sit at that table near the door," he said, "an' it wouldn't be a bad idea for you to do the same." He got up off the bar stool and walked over to this little table with two chairs at it. And I realized that the hundred proof bourbon was getting to him. But sometimes I take advice and I went over with him. I just didn't like the look of Cowboy Swensen tonight and I more than half believed the stories Rubberhose told about him. Besides, this was no time to get myself mixed up in a brawl. Not in Kansas and me being from New York City.

There was a commotion at the door right next to us and the screen door opened and this state trooper or highway patrolman came in. I don't know which. He had these butterfly pants and the broad-brimmed type hat on. He was a big fella with a kind of a round face, and it looked to me like under that hat he had a drill sergeant's haircut. He just stood there looking over the crowd kind of squinting. The place got a little quieter. The hillbilly band stopped playing. Cowboy had straightened up and was looking at the trooper. His head was tilted a little down and he sort of glared at the trooper.

"Ever'thin' goin' alright, Cowboy?" the trooper said. "Ever'body behavin' theirself?"

"Fly off outa here, Riddick," Cowboy said. "You got no call to come in here."

"Why, I ain't been by here in more'n a month, Cowboy," Riddick said. "I thought you'd be purely glad to see me."

"I come out from behind this bar, you gonna know how glad I am to see you," Cowboy said.

"You come out from behind that bar except I tell you," Riddick said, "I'll blow your goddam head off. You ain't got tubby old Pete McComb to protect you no more."

"I never needed no protection, Riddick," Cowboy said. His face was flushed and his hands were balled into huge knobby fists. "You take that gun off and I'll break you into little pieces. Now, you get on out of here before I do it anyway." The trooper didn't move. He grinned at Cowboy.

"C'mon, Cowboy!" he taunted. "Come at me. I won't kill you. I'll just put you in the hospital and then you'll go to jail. You're a crazy man, Cowboy. You don't belong out of no cage."

Cowboy's lady came over taking quick, tiny steps.

"Leave him a-goddamn alone!" she shrieked. "I'm gonna call your boss and tell him what you're trying to do! That's what I'm gonna do!"

"You're a sissy, Riddick!" Cowboy yelled. "Yellow. You need a gun to go up against Cowboy. Ain't no men left in Kansas. On'y sissies with guns. You ask Trooper McComb. Ask him what he thinks of the likes of you. He never needed no gun. He stood up to me. I whipped him. Whipped him good. But I respected him. All he ever had to do after I whipped him was ask. He didn't have to come strutting in like a goddamn rooster with a badge. You ask Pete McComb. He was a man. Now, get out of my place, sonny!"

The trooper kept his smile on like it was carved there. He looked around the room slowly, like he wanted to show everyone there that he was in charge and they better not forget it. After a minute he pointed his finger at Cowboy.

"Give me an excuse, Cowboy," he said. "It don't have to be a big one." He waited another second, patted Cowboy's girlfriend on the cheek and went out.

"Goddam sissy!" Cowboy yelled.

Rubberhose was quiet next to me. Then he said, "Think I'll go to my room and go to bed. It ain't fun no more." He got up and almost fell. I grabbed at him but he caught himself.

"You're too damn drunk to drive," I told him.

"Then I'll sleep in my car 'til I'm able," he said. He pushed through the screen door before I could stop him. Now he had me worried. Him and the way things just felt there in The Cascades. The place was dead quiet. Everybody was looking at Cowboy. His girlfriend went over to the bar.

"Go back to work!" Cowboy said to her. He looked toward the bandstand. "Who tol' you to stop playing? That's what I'm payin' you for!" The trooper must have put his siren on just to stick it to Cowboy a little more. A handsome guy at the table next to the bandstand stood up. His legs was spread apart and he held up a bottle of beer.

"Whyncha take his gun away from him, Cowboy?" he yelled. "You scared of a little ol' popgun, Cowboy?"

I don't remember exactly how things went right after that. I heard the siren going right away. Someone said, "Jesus Christ Almighty!" Cowboy come over the bar like he was on springs and went for the guy at the table next to the bandstand. He didn't make no sound that I can remember. I never seen a big guy like him move so quick. He made a beeline. It didn't make no difference if there was people or tables between him and whoever he was after. He knocked a guy off a stool. Tables, chairs, people, bottles went every which way. Girls started screaming. A lady with blue hair got knocked down. Her husband fell down trying to pick her up. And then people started heading for the door. I got there first.

It was quiet in the parking lot, which was about as big as half a football field and covered with cinders, and right now there were forty or fifty cars and pickups parked around the edges, leaving a big space in the middle. Like I said, The Cascades was built out of concrete block and that kept the noise pretty much inside. But when the people started to try to squeeze through that door three at a time, everything went crazy. Ladies were screaming and men were cursing and shoving each other. Pretty soon, maybe about three minutes later, there were fifteen or twenty people in the parking lot and this guy about fifty was holding his eyeglasses, which were broken, and holding his wife by the arm, which she had only one shoe.

"My shoe!" she hollered over and over.

"What about my goddamn eyeglasses?" he yelled. "I could have been blinded. It's a goddamn disgrace! That man's a maniac!"

"We didn't have to come here!" his wife said.

"You wanted to!" he shouted. "YOU! NOT ME! FUN, YOU SAID!"

"They oughta shoot that animal!" someone else said, "He's looney!"

That was only some of what I remember hearing. You got to understand that everybody was talking at once. And screaming and cursing. But not everybody came out of there. I was still at the edge of the parking lot. You could hear a lot of noise now from inside. The hillbilly band must of got out the back door, they come tearing around to the parking lot and started to get into this old Army bus that was still painted olive drab with the numbers painted over in black paint.

"What's going on there?" someone else yelled.

"Someone's gonna get killed!" one of the band guys said. "I seen someone waving a gun!" There was a shot right after that and more people began rushing through the door again and a lot of the people outside ran behind cars, including me. And the screams and cursing started all over again. Then there was another shot. It was a heavier shot. Like a shotgun. Not a boom! like they do in the movies but a sound like two thick boards slapped together. Then it was quiet. I never heard a quiet like that since the war. Jesus! It was scary! And then we all heard Cowboy.

"Down on the floor!" he shouted inside. "Everybody! Down on the goddamn floor!"

"What are you gonna do, Cowboy?" a female voice said. It was a whiney voice and I figured it was Cowboy's girlfriend.

"I dunno," Cowboy said. "Lock the back door!"

"But he's dead!" the girlfriend said. "What are you gonna do about him?"

"Lock the back door!" Cowboy shouted.

There was that quiet again. Then all the lights inside went out but the outside lights stayed on. I could hear crying from inside.

"Did anybody call the police?" someone near me shouted.

"There's no phone," someone else said.

Car engines started and this pickup tore out of the parking lot whiles two more pulled out. I was looking for Rubberhose. He was in the back seat of his great big 1937 Packard. I shook him awake and told him what was going on.

"It don't make no difference to me," he said. "It ain't fun no more." He got into the front seat and got the engine going. "Maybe I'll see you again sometime," he said. "Been nice knowing you. I don't want no part of this." He drove away and I haven't seen him from that day to this.

Rubberhose wasn't out of the parking lot a half a minute when I heard the police sirens. It wasn't Trooper Riddick but two others. They come screaming into the lot and was out of the car before it stopped and was hauling out their pistols. At least they was smart. They didn't go busting in there right away. Then they heard someone yell that Cowboy had a gun. They stopped and looked at each other. Then one of them went up beside the door.

"Hey, Cowboy!" he yelled. "What the hell are you up to?"

"Don't try to come in here!" Cowboy yelled. "I'll surely kill you."

"You got people in there, Cowboy," the trooper said. "They ain't no part of this!" There was silence.

"Someone got shot!" a man in the crowd yelled.

"Cowboy!" the trooper yelled. "Don't be foolish!" But Cowboy didn't answer him.

The two troopers talked together for a minute. The first one went back beside the door.

"Come on out, Cowboy," the trooper yelled. "I guarantee nothing will happen to you." But Cowboy didn't say a word. "How many people you got in there?"

"Don't know," Cowboy said. "Fifteen, twenty. Fifty maybe. I don't know! I don't care! You stay the goddam hell out!"

Then Riddick showed up with his siren on. He had his gun out and was all for going right in. But the other two troopers stopped him.

"I can handle that crazy son of a bitch!" Riddick said.

"He shot somebody," one of the troopers said. That changed Riddick's mind.

Well, it wasn't ten minutes before there was about fifteen police cars and I never seen so many guns. They brought searchlights and trained them on the front door. They went up the roof and tried the back door and the windows. But that place was a blockhouse. There was only one way in and one way out.

The crowd built up pretty quick and the cops had a hell of a time keeping them back. And all you heard was how they oughta hang Cowboy or fill him full of lead and like that.

And then someone mentioned this Pete McComb.

"He's retired," a trooper said.

"And he lives 'way in hell-an'-up in Mitchell County!" another said. "That's two hundred miles. Maybe two fifty. He don't even have a telephone."

A trooper with major's leaves on his shoulders said something to another trooper, who took off in his car.

There was no television there but there was newspaper reporters and a guy from the radio station.

I kind of sidled over to see if I could hear what was goin' on. The major was saying they was sending an airplane up for this Pete McComb and they would bring him down if they had to tie him up to do it, and they had already telephoned ahead to a barracks up near where this Pete McComb lived. It would take about two, three hours to get him down.

I remember wondering if somebody was hurt bad inside. The Cascades, what were they going to do about that? Somebody could die. I guess somebody else thought about that too because a couple of ambulances showed up. There was nothing for the guys on the ambulances to do except wait.

I got a little bit of buzz on sitting inside The Cascades, but it was all gone now and I was feeling pretty rotten the way you do. And I still had to get back to my rooming house, which was a couple of miles away. I didn't know if I wanted to stick around to see what happened or get out of there. More and more people were showing up in the parking lot now, even though it was about midnight and, like the beginning with people standing around joking or just being mad about what was going on, they were doing the same thing. Only it was worse like "Cowboy's giving that part of Kansas a bad name" and "They ought to do something about him and his like."

It was maybe three o'clock in the morning when this Pete McComb showed up. They landed at Boeing on the airfield there and drove him in a cruiser to The Cascades. It looked like a lot of people knew him from before. He was a big guy about fifty and he was wearing khaki pants and a short-sleeve shirt and a cowboy hat that was pretty beat up. He had that tough deadface look you see on cops all over and he talked with the major for a few minutes. He didn't bother with the people in the crowd who were yelling to him. Except once. He looked the crowd over.

"For Christ sake!" he yelled. "Go home and let us do our job without nobody gets hurt!" But nobody paid attention. "They wanna see somebody get killed," he said to the major.

McComb went up to the side of the door and yelled to Cowboy.

"Hey, Cowboy!" he said. "It's me, McComb. Kin I come in?"

There was no answer for a minute.

"I trust you, McComb!" Cowboy yelled.

"Then put on the lights and let me come in!" McComb said. "No tricks. You got my word." McComb pointed at the major and nodded his head. The major waited a second and nodded his head back. The lights went on. McComb stood full in the doorway and then went inside. After a minute he came out.

"There's two shot people in there," he said "One of 'em's dead. The othern's pretty bad." He pointed to the ambulance people. "You can come in and get 'em." As they started to move, the major held a pistol toward McComb. McComb shook his head. "I give my word," he said, and went back inside. The ambulance people followed him in. After a while they came out with two people on stretchers. One was all wrapped up in a gray blanket, even his head, and I couldn't see who it was. But there wasn't no doubt he was the one who got killed. The other was a guy I seen at the table next to the bandstand, only his face was showing and he had that pasty, eyes-half-open look, and I seen enough of that kind of thing to know that he would not be around very much longer.

This Pete McComb came out right behind them and stood in the doorway. He watched while the stretchers was put into the ambulances and they took off. The major went up to McComb.

"Cowboy says he didn't shoot nobody," McComb said to him. "He went after that dead lad like he always does and that dead lad pulled a gun but he hit his friend instead of Cowboy. I can't get the straight out of it how somebody got Cowboy's shotgun. But somebody did and blowed the other one's head half away."

The major stood there a minute. "We can figure it all out later," he said finally. "Just get that squirrelly jerk out of there."

"Well," McComb said very calm, "he's got that shotgun and all them people in there. Besides, he wants to fight me—or him." He pointed to Riddick. Riddick looked like he was scared to death they would send him in.

"Can't have that," the major said.

"No," McComb said, "can't have that. Besides, he'd kill Riddick."

"Well?" the major said.

"Anybody got a jack?" McComb asked.

"You know we ain't allowed to carry them things," the major said. McComb just looked at him. The major talked to a trooper who went over to a car and came back with this blackjack, which he tried to hide up the cuff of his shirt. McComb kind of palmed it and didn't say one more word but went back inside The Cascades. It got quiet again. Dead quiet. You could hear engines being run up on the test blocks down at Boeing it was so quiet.

Then there was this awful scream. A screech more like. And then the shotgun went off again. And more screeching.

"Shut the goddam hell up!" It was McComb's voice. The screeching stopped. "Git a man in here!" McComb yelled. The major pointed to Riddick maybe because he was the closest and Riddick hauled out his pistol, which looked like a .45 caliber revolver with bone handles, and went crashing through the screen door.

"Put that goddam thing away!" McComb yelled. There was nothing more for maybe a minute and then Riddick came out looking very businesslike.

"Everybody has to stand back!" he yelled. "They're comin' out." But the crowd pushed forward.

"Hang the son of a bitch!" someone yelled and the whole crowd started yelling at once. The major gave a signal and the troopers and the other cops started to push the people back. Then Cowboy and McComb came out. Cowboy had his shirt off. Or most of it. All he had on was the collar and one cuff. He had this big scrape across his chest that was bleeding. And he had this wild, desperate look on his face. His hands were cuffed behind him. McComb held the shotgun in the crook of his arm. It was broke open and wasn't loaded.

They stood in the doorway for a minute. Cowboy's girlfriend was behind them with her hands up to her mouth. Her hair was all down and she looked scared as hell. There was other people behind her but nobody tried to get out just then.

It's funny how a crowd gets quiet at times like that. He was handcuffed and there was all these cops with guns around, but all those people were scared of Cowboy. I mean, *scared*! And Cowboy grinned at them could because he knew it.

"They had to use a blackjack on ol' Cowboy!" he yelled. "I ain't never been licked fair yet. Never! They had to put ol' Cowboy down with a blackjack!"

"Git!" McComb said to Cowboy, and gave him a little shove. Cowboy turned like he was going to butt McComb. Riddick cocked his fist and whammed Cowboy on the side of the head, and that set the crowd to yelling. But Cowboy didn't go down. He turned and kicked Riddick right in the balls. Riddick let out a yell and fell down and Cowboy went to stomp him. The crowd was really all worked up now and the cops were having a hell of a time trying to keep them back. And Cowboy was yelling too.

"Shit-for-brains Riddick!" he yelled. He was trying to stomp Riddick, and McComb had a hold of the handcuff links and was pulling him back and having a hard time doing it. The crowd was yelling and pushing, and then there came this little bitty *crack*! and Cowboy just dropped.

Now, you seen a lot of people get killed in movies and they do dances and throw out their arms or stand with this dopey look for half a goddamn hour before they go down or they get blown back maybe a hundred feet and like that. It don't happen that way and it didn't with Cowboy. He just dropped like he was dead, and anybody who seen the real thing like in the war knew it. Cowboy Swensen who never lost a rough-and-tumble fight in his life was killed dead by some guy in the crowd who stuck a shiny nickel-plated .25 caliber automatic, it turned out later, up near Cowboy's head and fired one shot. And Cowboy Swensen was as dead as if he'd been hit direct by a round from a German eighty-eight.

Well, they got the guy. Somebody grabbed his arm right after he shot Cowboy and held on, and the cops worked him over somewhat while they were subduing him. I never got a look at him. All I saw was this major and Pete McComb standing looking down at Cowboy Swensen while the ruckus was going on all around and McComb shaking his head.

That finished Kansas for me for good. And that letter from my ex about gettin' married to the fireman settled things as far as between going back to New York and going to California. I picked up my pay and got a bus ticket for San Francisco, which they told me was as close to New York as you could get, which I don't agree. It's pretty and it's got hills but it ain't New York.

I got work right away and pretty soon I forgot about Cowboy Swensen. I even stopped wonderin' what happened to The Cascades or Cowboy's girlfriend or the guy on the stretcher if he died or not or if they did anything to the one who shot Cowboy. But I never forgot the last time I seen Rubberhose and how he said it wasn't no fun no more. And it wasn't. I went up and down the coast of California always workin', always making good money. And I met my share of ladies and some of them was pretty nice. But I wasn't having no fun. I don't mean laugh-it-up fun but like enjoyment. I mean, nothing was really happening for me. And then Korea came and I went back in the Army for some reason.

There's that saying about going to the well once too often. I was with the 529th Engineering Battalion attached to the First Cavalry. I made staff sergeant and was really feeling pretty good and thinking I'd stay in the Army. It wasn't such a bad life if you kept your sense of humor.

Christ! I remember so clear that day. It was my birthday. I was twenty-eight and I was supposed to get rotated back to Seoul the next day. I was sitting with these guys and I remember talkin' to one of the guys, a guy from South Boston who always had a snappy comeback for anything.

"I got half a mind to get married again," I remember saying.

"That's all you need," my friend from South Boston said. And everybody laughed. And the next thing I knew someone yells, "INCOMING!"

I never even got a chance to move. A Chink shell must of dropped right in our laps. I heard South Boston got killed outright. Two other guys got killed. I don't remember feeling a thing. Nothing! And I ain't felt nothing from the waist down ever since.

What I'm getting around to is people don't know what's inside your head. And they don't really give a good goddamn. I mean, they been pretty good to me in the vets hospitals. They done all they could, I guess. But after a while you're like part of the furniture. They forget you can think and feel and they really don't want to listen, even if I could talk.

That's why I'm writin' this all down. Maybe somebody will read it, if I let them.

That poor guy I told you about up front. And Cowboy Swensen. I know what they been through. I mean, I think they was just tryin' to get even.

Jesus Christ! I wish there was some way I could.

THE CHRISTMAS TREE

THE CHRISTMAS TREE

Where I grew up in New York City—a neighborhood we'll call Northvale—hasn't changed a whole lot over the past fifty years. I can attest to that because I find myself in the old neighborhood on occasion. Not for any particular reason. I'm usually passing through on my way from one place to another, infrequently enough that I would readily notice changes. There are a few new apartment buildings. The Masonic Hall has been replaced by a school building. Brick two-family row houses have sprung up in what were empty lots. There's a teenage hangout just about where it's always been, but it's a pizzeria now instead of an ice cream parlor. Sometimes something will strike me, and I will park the car and walk a bit through the older, quiet streets banked with tight little houses with their patches of green in front and narrow driveways leading to detached one-car garages and surprisingly generous backyards.

Those houses were there when my family first came to Northvale in the late twenties. Of course, Northvale is not the real name of that tiny enclave of respectability. If you know New York City at all, or the Bronx specifically, you'll probably guess the exact location, and you might even have lived there and remember some of what will follow. But most of the principals are gone now, dead or moved away. I'm pretty sure that there is no person still in Northvale who would have direct knowledge of, or involvement in, the matter of Jimmy Swift and Patrick James McCaffrey and a magnificent Christmas tree. At least I hope that's the case.

My uncle Martin used to say that in a place like Northvale—and I'm not happy with that name, but it will have to do—there were three main religious faiths: Jewish, Christian, and Roman Catholic. The Jews were undeniably not Christian. But the Catholics seemed to believe that a baptized Catholic was also not a Christian, and vice versa. There was and is no Jewish house of worship in Northvale, although there have always been Jewish families. There were four churches: the Catholic church and school of St. Michael the Archangel (another alias), and three churches of the Protestant persuasion. But Northvale was predominantly Catholic—Irish and Italian mostly, with loose change of other European origins. It was also a blue uniform community, so many of the families were headed by police or firemen. There were railroaders as well, and ironworkers and bus and trolley drivers and letter carriers. There were also teachers and shopkeepers and doctors and lawyers and office workers. It was a place where married women stayed home and single girls "went to business" with the telephone company or an insurance company.

There were some in Northvale who were considered poor. But that was more a matter of perception than reality. It would be a misrepresentation, especially in the depths of the Depression, to say that no families were receiving public assistance or gifts of food and clothing collected and distributed at Easter and Christmas by St. Michael the Archangel or the St. Vincent de Paul Society. Even the Protestants "lent a hand" to their own distressed.

We didn't really know what "rich" meant. The people who lived in the large brick homes with lush shrubbery and glorious oak and elm trees, carefully tended lawns with wrought-iron lawn furniture painted white, were not considered rich but well-off, or well-to-do.

One of those families was the Patrick James McCaffreys, or The McCaffrey, as P.J. preferred to be called. They lived in a huge

Victorian home on a corner plot that was twice the size of any other plot in Northvale. The house was well set back from the street. The plot itself was a good four feet higher than the sidewalk and was buttressed on two sides by a well-constructed retaining wall of native granite topped with sharp stones set into a layer of cement. A driveway curved up from the street across the front of the house and back down to the street. A three-car garage behind the house was accessible from a side street. A white-painted iron gate with the McCaffrey heraldic shield riveted to each center panel kept out intruders. The gate was fashioned by an Irish blacksmith brought over from Ireland by P.J.

A magnificent old blue spruce stood in awesome symmetry at the corner of the McCaffrey "estate." I did not at the time, nor did any of my friends, know that the big tree was a blue spruce. To us, it was a Christmas tree, the tallest, fullest Christmas tree I had ever seen. Even when I joined the Boy Scouts and went camping in "the woods," I never saw a tree as beautiful as P.J. McCaffrey's Christmas tree. And I was not alone. As hated and feared as P.J. was in Northvale—and probably everywhere he went or had been—that tree was admired by any who saw it. I would like to be able to say exactly how tall it was. My memory flashes the number fifty and sometimes scales that down to thirty-five. But remembering the house and where the top of the tree reached, I would have to settle on eighteen to twenty feet high and seven feet across at the base. The McCaffreys came to Northvale after my family did, and I realize now that P.J. couldn't have planted that tree as a seedling. Charley Farrell, who knew something about trees and bushes from the time he worked in a nearby cemetery, said, whenever the subject of the Christmas tree came up, that P.J. had swiped it from a park in Scarsdale when it was a third the size that I remember.

P.J. himself was as imposing as his house. He was tall, barrel-chested, and square-shouldered. His eyebrows were thick and black as coal, and his hair, cropped close, was as white as snow. His face was square, thin-lipped, and ruddy. His eyes were sky blue and hard. He was, my uncle Tim on my mother's side told me, a Kerry man, and I've spent the rest of my life since then believing that anyone born in County Kerry was born angry, for that was how Pat McCaffrey always appeared to me.

I should mention that my only personal contact with P.J. was when I was still a kid on my way to get a haircut at Mr. Penucchio's barber shop on a Saturday morning. I always got my hair cut on a Saturday morning. This one morning, I got to the barber shop just as P.J. was coming out. He wore, as always, a tweed jacket and corduroy pants—we used to call them "whistle britches" because of the noise they made when you walked. He also wore an old gray fedora that made him look taller than he was. He made me think of the leathery "cattle barons" I used to see in the old-time Western movies. P.J. always walked with long strides, leaning forward a bit as if into a wind. I never saw him in Northvale except when he was walking that driving walk of his.

This morning, his face was redder than usual.

"Hello, lad," he growled at me as he went by. I think I said "Hello" as well.

Mr. Penucchio was stropping a straight razor as I came in. He was not looking at what he was doing but glaring out the window. He had the sheet or whatever it's called ready before I got my windbreaker off and motioned me to the chair.

He was talking in that crazy Sicilian dialect of his. I just sat there, trying to get a look at myself in the mirror or read the labels on all the bottles on the shelf under the mirror. I could always tell almost to the split-second when Mr. Penucchio was finished with my cut. He would slick my hair down, powder the back of my neck with a towel, and whip off the sheet. This particular morning, he took my fifty cents without a word, which was unusual for him. I watched him put the coins in his ancient cash register. He seemed to have forgotten that I was in the shop. He looked out to the street. "Summa-day," he said slowly and clearly, "I'm gonna cut off his goddamn head!" I knew it was P.J. he was talking about.

I told my father about it. He laughed.

"Mr. McCaffrey doesn't like Italians, and Mr. Penucchio doesn't like Irishmen," he explained. He thought a moment. "No—that's not right. Mr. Penucchio doesn't like Mr. McCaffrey."

The McCaffreys had four daughters. The eldest was Maura, who was married to a lawyer and lived someplace else. The other three—Rosemary, Eileen, and Margaret Mary—were each about a year and a half apart in age. Rosemary went from high school into the convent, which, my father had said, "got Pat Mac off the hook." I asked him what he meant.

"With some of the old Irish," he explained, "get a Roman collar or a nun's habit on one of your kids, it's a free pass into heaven."

"You were born in Ireland," I reminded him. "Do you believe that?"

We were two boys and a girl, and I was number three. My brother and sister were in high school, and there was no sign that either of them felt a call to the cloth. I know I didn't. But maybe he had plans for me.

"Jamesie," he said, "I came over to America with nothin' in my poke but lint because I wanted to live my own life in my own way. I wouldn't be much of a man to deny that right to any of my children, would I?"

Well, maybe P.J. got his free pass, and maybe he didn't. The lawyer Maura married was a Protestant, so that could have canceled out Rosemary's calling. What everybody knew was that P.J. had read Maura out of the family and forbade anyone to say her name in his presence or to have any communication with her. He did not even recognize her children as his grandchildren. Of course, he still had two other daughters to sacrifice to the Church and ensure his salvation. And he guarded them with the ferocity of a bull elephant. Eileen was seventeen and beautiful. Every guy I knew thought it would be a crying shame for her to waste that beauty on the Church. But that was what almost everyone was convinced would happen. It was a time when girls wore hats and white gloves, and she was the only one I ever thought didn't look downright stupid in a hat. Her clothes were always expensive, and she knew how to wear them. I wasn't the only altar boy who wanted to be the one to hold the communion plate under that perfect chin. If she would only look up—just once. But she never did, no matter what the other guys claimed.

You could bet that the last guy in the world who would have a chance with Eileen McCaffrey was Jimmy Swift. Jimmy was good-looking, tall, and slender. He was something of a track star in high school and won an athletic scholarship to some college. But his parents wouldn't let him accept it. Jimmy was never an altar boy. His father was an atheist, and his mother was a Socialist. Jimmy was an only child and went to public school. He was also what they called—the adults—a "latchkey kid." The consensus was that Jimmy would probably wind up a criminal or a Communist. If he was embarrassed by his parents or if he was proud of them, you never could tell. His life was none of your business. But Jimmy Swift always had a crush on Eileen. He never said so—Jimmy was a quiet guy—but he'd go goofy every time she was anywhere nearby.

Jimmy, good with his hands, was a first-rate mechanic before he turned eighteen. When he got out of high school, he went to work in his father's gas station, which was in the neighborhood. That was where P.J. McCaffrey had his cars serviced. And because of that, Jimmy was the only guy I knew who saw Eileen regularly and even got to talk to her without P.J. climbing all over him. It probably never occurred to P.J. that he had anything to fear from a practically invisible grease monkey like Jimmy Swift. But Jimmy Swift's father noticed the signs of a coming storm and advised his son to watch himself. He didn't. What mattered to him more than anything was to win the affection of Eileen McCaffrey. Jimmy was only nineteen when the trouble started.

When the Spanish Civil War broke out in 1936, Jimmy Swift's father went to Spain to fight with the Loyalists against Franco. His mother went around making speeches on street corners. The only solace Jimmy got out of life was seeing and talking with Eileen when he would deliver one or another of P.J.'s cars. Then a miracle happened. At least Jimmy saw it that way. P.J.'s construction business began to pick up. He'd gotten a couple of contracts from the city, and he needed a driver to take him to the various sites. Jimmy got to see and talk to Eileen every day. He was wary of P.J., of course. He might have been gaga with love for Eileen, but he wasn't stupid. Then came the Christmas of 1937.

Every Christmas, P.J. would have that magnificent blue spruce festooned with electric lights of every color and shape, and angels, snowmen, tiny cottages, reindeer, Japanese lanterns, and dazzling ornaments imported from Germany. On top of the tree would be an oversized starburst of gold and white. It took several of his workmen three days to decorate it. That year, Jimmy Swift was one of them. His father would have raised hell about it had he been around, but his mother was too busy fomenting revolution in the Bronx.

It had become a tradition that many of the parishioners of St. Michael the Archangel would gather after Midnight Mass to sing carols around P.J.'s tree. A number of the choir members would be on the porch, leading the singing under the direction of the choirmaster and organist. P.J. even invited the pastors and congregations of the Protestant churches to join in. P.J. would roar out the hymns from his porch vantage point while his daughters and his wife, Kathleen, served hot cocoa to the gathered songsters. Despite the general feeling of hostility to P.J., the evening was usually a happy one.

The singing always began at about one thirty a.m. Christmas morning. A crèche was set in front of the tree. Around it were the figures of Mary and Joseph, shepherds, and farm animals. The manger, however, would be empty. Just before the final hymn, which was always "Adeste Fideles," P.J. would enter the house to get the Infant, which he would then carry to the tree and place gently and reverently in the crèche. The choir would explode into song, joined by the crowd.

On this particular night, as the notes of the next-to-last hymn, "Hark the Herald Angels Sing," faded, P.J. had already departed the porch to retrieve the Infant. But two minutes passed, and he had not reappeared. Then Kathleen entered the house. Thirty seconds later, they both came out, followed by Eileen. Mrs. McCaffrey's face was grim. P.J.'s was flushed. He carried the Infant in one huge paw like a log of wood and all but dumped the figure into the crèche. Then the entire McCaffrey clan rushed back into the house. The singing of the crowd waned. The choir forged ahead. Everybody looked puzzled and began to drift slowly away. Snow began to fall, and some of the crowd started singing "Jingle Bells" as they left the vicinity of P.J. McCaffrey's house.

It was New Year's Day before anyone learned what had happened. The story came from Jimmy Swift himself. When P.J. had entered the house for the Infant, he caught Jimmy and Eileen embracing at the foot of the stairs. Jimmy had just given her his Christmas present, a pretty compact containing face powder and lip rouge. It had cost him six dollars. P.J. swung at Jimmy as the two lovers parted and knocked him to the floor. He ordered Jimmy out of the house through a back door. He would have struck Eileen, but Kathleen had entered the house in time to prevent it.

That should have ended things. But neither P.J. nor Jimmy would have it that way. Jimmy persisted in trying to see Eileen, to communicate with her any way he could. He looked for an ally, an intermediary. He even tried to recruit Eileen's sister, Margaret Mary, but she was frightened of her father.

I think his only friend was my older brother, Kenny. As much as the neighborhood disliked P.J., there wasn't much sympathy for Jimmy either on account of his parents. But Kenny couldn't help with Eileen. Besides, Jimmy was the kind of guy who rowed his own boat.

One day towards spring, Jimmy confronted P.J. on the street. He told P.J. he wanted to marry Eileen. P.J. sent Jimmy to the ground with a backhand. Jimmy got up quickly, but P.J. had turned his back in contempt and strode away. Jimmy did nothing. He didn't chase P.J. He didn't curse him. He simply stood, frozen with shame and anger, and then ran home.

Later that week, Jimmy came to see my father. He wanted to join the Army and needed a reference. My father saw no reason not to vouch for Jimmy. The next day, Jimmy went down to the Army Building on Whitehall Street. The only one to see him off was Kenny. It wasn't until six months later that Kenny got a letter from Jimmy, saying he was in the Panama Canal Zone in the Army Air Corps and working as an airplane mechanic.

Eileen McCaffrey went on to college, a Catholic women's college in upstate New York. The people of Northvale forgot all about Jimmy Swift and his father and mother. Someone heard that the father had been wounded in the fighting in Spain and was in Russia. Nobody knew what happened to Jimmy's mother.

A year passed. Another Christmas season came and went with no incidents at the ceremony around P.J.'s Christmas tree. Eileen came home for that Christmas. She looked sad and, unbelievably, drab. Margaret Mary said Eileen hardly spoke to her or to her mother and not at all to her father.

I don't remember when I first noticed a change in P.J. It was probably after I began to go steady, more or less, with Margaret Mary, which was something of a shocker in itself. Megs, as she was called, had molted her tomboy image by her junior year in high school. The school she went to, an all-girl academy run by nuns, was near the school I was going to. We would meet on the bus on the way home. I think that parents, Catholic ones at least, really believed that a Catholic educational environment insulated students from the evils of sexuality. In any event, P.J., although grumpy about my attentions to his daughter and apparently resigned to the certainty that Margaret Mary was not destined for the habit, allowed us to date with severe and rigid guidelines. We behaved ourselves, but Margaret Mary was not in the least any longer intimidated by her father. We got along very well and married when I got out of the service in 1945. But that's a different story.

Megs would say very little about Eileen back then. I began to believe that they did not get along or even like each other. Certainly, they had very different personalities. Everything became explosively clear during Christmas week of 1939.

The war in Europe had broken out in September. My brother had gotten an appointment to the United States Naval Academy and was in his second year. He came home on Christmas leave and told me he'd gotten a letter from Jimmy Swift, saying Jimmy would be back in Northvale for Christmas. Jimmy said he had been accepted for Officer Candidate School and would be on furlough until the first week of January. Kenny was home for a couple of days, and Jimmy Swift had not yet appeared. My whole family went to Midnight Mass together for the first time in two years. And we all agreed we'd sing carols around P.J.'s Christmas tree afterward.

In the church, we all waited for the appearance of the McCaffrey family. They finally showed up, but without Eileen. They were a glum bunch, except for Megs. She whacked me on the arm as the parade passed our pew. Something was up.

After Mass, we all trooped out and stood about the church steps in the cold and the new fallen snow, exchanging greetings with neighbors and friends. Still no sign of Jimmy. Not that anyone expected him to attend Mass.

By one thirty, we had arrived at the McCaffreys. The tree lights were out—which was certainly unusual—and there was no sign of the family. The choir arrived late. There was a confused hubbub among the growing throng of carolers. The crowd was bigger than it ever was, probably because of the war. A flustered P.J. finally came onto the porch, followed by Kathleen and Margaret Mary. He raised his arms.

"I want you to be quiet!" he shouted in his thick Kerry brogue. His order did nothing to settle things down. "Everything will go off fine! I apologize for the lights—there's a broken connection, and I think I know where it is! Now—hold off on the singing till I fix it!" More hubbub. P.J. came down the steps and got to his knees at the base of the tree. After a moment, he stood up again, flashlight in one hand and an electrical wire in the other. He followed the wire to the base of the porch and held up the unplugged end of it. "Here it is! I told you! We'll all be singing in a minute!"

As P.J. spoke, I was surprised to see a car, a Model A Ford coupe, approaching the crowd from the direction of the church. It stopped a half block away. The driver turned off the headlights, I guessed to watch the festivities, but did not turn off the motor or leave the car.

"All ready, now," P.J. yelled, ready to relight the tree. He leaned down to reconnect the wire to an extension cord. The lights came on—for a split second. There was a flash and a loud report like a giant firecracker, then a billow of smoke from the base of the tree. Gasps came up from the crowd, then silence. Almost imperceptibly, P.J.'s Christmas tree began to lean toward the street. Then the screams and shouts started. The tree fell irretrievably with gathering force and crashed hard to the ground, its starburst decoration skittering off into the road. Again, there was silence. A stunned silence. P.J. looked as if he'd been shot.

"P.J. McCaffrey!" came a shout. It was Jimmy Swift. He stood next to the Ford coupe, and beside him was Eileen. He was in uniform and looked about twenty pounds heavier. Eileen huddled against him.

"I want you to meet my wife, you son of a bitch!"

Then Jimmy and Eileen got back into the car. Jimmy turned the car around and slowly drove onto the side street. Eileen did not turn her head to look at the house she had lived in most of her life, or her family. I looked back at the ruined tree and then at P.J., standing with his mouth agape. I smelled an odor I would come to recognize—cordite. Jimmy must have booby-trapped the tree while the family was at Mass. Just enough powder to sever the tree trunk at the base. I saw Megs with her hand to her mouth. I couldn't tell if she was trying to suppress a laugh or a sob, though later she would explain.

Well, P.J. deserved it, but I felt sorry as hell for that lovely tree.

REUNION

REUNION

Michael settled himself in the rear seat of the taxi, intending to snooze a bit on the too-familiar and ever dull ride from National Airport to downtown Washington. He had made the trip enough times that he could pick out the new high-rise apartments, shopping malls, and government buildings that had risen on the landscape since his last visit. They were all of a drab and sterile sameness that aroused no interest. The wonder was that there was any room left to build anything. He was pleased that the reunion was to be held at the old and, he hoped, still graceful Wardman Park Hotel, now the Sheraton Park, on Connecticut Avenue. It had been years since he had stopped there. The Hay-Adams or The Mayflower were more convenient.

The last time he had stayed at the low, rambling Wardman Park was ten years ago, when he and Chrissie had come from New York for Billy's graduation from Georgetown. It was still the Wardman Park then.

The first time, though, in 1942, Michael had been worried that he would be caught and thrown out of the place by a burly house detective.

He had been on his way overseas with a provisional group of aircrews, replacements for the Eighth Air Force in England. The group was billeted at Camp Kilmer near New Brunswick, New Jersey, and the crews were on "red alert," which meant that they could move out at any time to board a troopship. Therefore, all personnel were restricted to the base.

Michael, then Second Lieutenant Michael Francis O'Reilly, United States Army Air Corps, had had no intention of observing the restriction. Home in the Bronx was a mere forty miles away, and he had not had leave since his aviation cadet days in Texas months earlier. He had arranged with a fellow pilot to contact him at his parents' if orders came through to move out. But when Michael called home, he learned that his parents were in Washington, where his father had been called to receive a presidential appointment to the War Production Board. So, he had headed his rental car south.

Washington was crammed then as he had never seen it. Michael caught up with his parents at the Willard Hotel just three hours before they were to take the train back to New York. They barely had time for a few drinks and a sandwich. It was an emotional time. Michael's mother had wept a bit, certain that she was seeing her eldest son for the last time. Michael's father had been hearty and cheerful.

"War is a terrible thing," he had said. "But if there is one, a young man ought not miss the opportunity to test himself. If one survives it, wartime service—combat—is the most thrilling experience of a lifetime."

They had parted shortly after at Union Station. Michael felt bereft and a little frightened. He had driven his parents to the station and parked his car just outside near the taxi ramp. When he came out, it seemed like hundreds of people were trying to get taxis. He offered to give lifts to a number of them going in his direction, north. He had decided that Washington held no attraction for him and that he might as well return to Camp Kilmer. There were too many uniforms in Washington, too much rank. As a second lieutenant, he felt self-conscious and intimidated.

Four riders accepted, one a WAAC lieutenant, who was billeted at the Wardman Park. What happened afterward, Michael assured himself, happened by pure chance. The WAAC officer—he had forgotten her name—was being let off last. He remembered how uncertain of himself he had been when the two of them were alone in the car. He had just turned twenty-one and he was sure—and he was right—that she was older than he, although not by much. She was from Louisiana and had been in the Army for a year and a half, about the same length of time as Michael. They were both a little more used to each other by the time they reached the Wardman Park. That was another observation of Michael's father. "War accelerates everything. Heightens every feeling. Magnifies every event. Intensifies every encounter. Destroys time."

Michael understood what he meant later. There had been drinks and dancing with the WAAC lieutenant, and then the night spent with her. There had been intensity, passion. Perhaps there even had been love. But there had been no time to find out. He left the WAAC's room at six o'clock in the morning and took the stairs to the farthest corner of the great lobby, expecting at any moment to be collared by the "house dick." But he had gotten out without incident and drove back to Camp Kilmer, arriving barely in time to pack his belongings and draw an issue of gas mask, steel helmet, and liner—for what reason, he could not fathom. From Kilmer, a train took the provisional group to Hoboken where, along with fifteen thousand soldiers, sailors, airmen, and civilians, they boarded the *Queen Mary* for a solo dash across the hostile North Atlantic.

It was strange, he thought, that the memory of that encounter with the WAAC lieutenant should surface now. He had not thought of her the other times he had stayed at the Wardman Park. *Something is happening*, he told himself in the taxi. And he realized that he had not answered Chrissie's question—even to himself—as to why he had elected to attend this particular reunion of the Eighth Air Force when he had shown no interest in attending the previous three.

"It's in Washington this year," he had said. "I can take care of some business and just drop by to see what's what. There might be some memorabilia and one or two people I served with."

"But as long as we've been married," Chrissie said, "you seldom spoke about the war. In fact, it seemed to upset you when it came up. Your medals are stuck away in a trunk."

That was true. Oh, there were times when he told his share of war stories. People used to want to know about combat and especially about his experience in a prisoner-of-war camp. But their interest had been vicarious, and he felt uncomfortable when he was asked to recall his experiences. He had never known how to present them. Not too many people had done a full tour of combat in Europe and then spent a year and a half in a German prison camp. He did not need to entertain, he would not, those whose youthful years were less spectacular. Then there was Korea and Viet Nam, and World War II faded into the mists. Nobody really cared anymore about what Michael O'Reilly had done in a war that was a generation and a half into the past.

So why now? Was his interest aroused simply because the reunion was being held in a city close enough to demand no special effort? It was true that there was always business to be done in Washington. Yet there was nothing really pressing enough to warrant a trip at this particular time. He could have come down the following week or the following month.

Michael placed his attaché case on his lap and opened it. He took out a file folder. Chrissie would have been surprised to see its contents. It held all of the material he had received relating to the past three Eighth Air Force reunions. He had not thrown it out as she had thought. He examined again the brochure for the current reunion. There was nothing in it that stuck in the mind. He closed the attaché case.

"Dammit!" he said half aloud.

The taxi driver, a man who appeared to be about Michael's age, cocked his head. "What?" he said.

"Just talking to myself," Michael said. He felt a need to give voice to his wonderment. "I can't figure out why, after thirty-five years, I've suddenly become interested in my old outfit."

"Yeah," the driver said. "That Air Corps thing. I took another passenger there last night. Me—I was in the infantry. Twenty-Eighth division. You can have it. I had a lousy time. Lousy. I don't even wanna think about it. If I was to see my old company commander crossing the street, I'd have all I could do to keep from running the son of a bitch down. A real no-good." The driver fell silent a moment. "Still," he went on, "I guess if things was good, you'd want to remember them. For me it was a lousy time. I don't want no part of it." He stopped for a light. Michael could see the entrance to the hotel a block away. The driver half turned in his seat.

"I don't want to spoil nothing for you," he said. "They used to say the end of the war cancels all debts. But I ain't so sure. There's a few guys still owe me, and I ain't talking about money. You know what I mean?"

And Michael did know what the driver meant. There was Joe S. Hardee, Captain Joe S. Hardee of Yuma, Arizona, and Michael realized that Hardee was one of the reasons he had decided to attend the fourth annual reunion of the Eighth Air Force. He would not have gone all the way out to St. Louis. Or to Dayton. Or to Ft. Lauderdale. Those were the cities where the three previous reunions had been held. He had to admit that he had considered attending the first one. He remembered when the invitation had come. It was the week after he had returned from London during a visit that coincided with a commemoration of the Battle of Britain. There had been an awe-inspiring flypast of ancient Spitfires and Hurricanes, and Michael had stood in Trafalgar Square, head tilted toward the sky, mouth agape in honest admiration.

"Beautiful!" he had said aloud.

A man standing next to him said, "I was ack-ack. I used to watch 'em. Gawd. What they done!" Then the flypast was over, and

Michael and the Londoner chatted a bit.

"I was here during the war," Michael said. "With the Eighth Air Force."

"Were you air crew?" the man asked.

"Pilot," Michael said.

"Fortressed?" the man asked—hopefully, Michael had thought.

"Yes," Michael said.

"Ah," the man said. "You lads did a fine job. Yes, indeed you did." Then the man walked away, and Michael had been left to wonder at his abrupt departure. He heard the heavy thrum of bombers and felt a tingle of excitement. He looked skyward, but the aircraft—they must have been Lancasters or Halifaxes—were hidden from his view. Later, over drinks, he and a London business associate had talked about the war, but mostly about the great times they had had in London on leave.

But Michael didn't go to St. Louis, or Ohio, or Ft. Lauderdale. Now, when he got news of this fourth reunion, he had felt an urge to attend. He was proud of his service, of his Silver Star and his Distinguished Flying Cross. Funny that his children had never asked about them, had never seemed curious about his days as a pilot in the greatest air force the world had ever seen. They watched those ridiculous war films on television and never once asked what it was really like, and they groused at him or twitted him when he insisted on watching the documentaries. He treasured his war, if the truth were known. Chrissie never suspected it, and he was always disinclined to boast. Now he was giving in to the impulse to reach back into those days of glory, and still there was the question of "Why now?" Was it Joe S. Hardee? Had he, Michael O'Reilly, harbored that resentment, that anger for all these years? Maybe the cab driver was right. There are some wartime debts that can never be cancelled.

His reverie was interrupted by the taxi's arrival at the main entrance to the hotel.

"Have a good time," the driver said as Michael paid him. "It was a pretty good war for some."

Michael noted with some dismay that in the morning sun, the former Wardman Park was looking tatty. He noticed some construction vehicles parked on the side. On one was a large sign with a rendering of the new building that was even then being built within the center court of the old hotel. *Another set of boxes*, Michael thought. *Lord*, he thought, *must something be a monument before "they" would leave it alone?* He went inside and saw that the lobby had been changed enough to make it an unsightly hybrid, and for a moment he thought that he might have made a mistake in coming. Would it be the same with the men he had served with? Would they look tatty and worn out? Would they be like so many men his age he had seen, togged out in young men's clothing, hair tinted to hide the gray?

The lobby was nearly empty. It was still at least an hour before the reunion registration desk would be open. He went directly to the front desk. He had made his own reservation, a small suite in the Wardman Tower. He had decided to wait until he actually arrived at the hotel before committing himself. He wanted to see what sort of crowd would show up.

He went up to the suite and considered calling Chrissie and urging her to join him. No. He would wait. He might be leaving even before the reunion got under way.

He opened his attaché for the schedule of events. There were a couple of cocktail "get-togethers," a breakfast, and two dinners, the final one a gala with dancing afterwards. His own group, the 612th Bomb Group, would hold its own "mini-reunion," and a "hospitality suite" would be open each day for "hangar flying and renewing old friendships." If Captain Joe S. Hardee attended the reunion, it was probable that he would be found most easily at the hospitality suite.

And if he was there, then what? What would happen if he walked into the hospitality suite and encountered Hardee? Would there be anyone in the room who knew the reason why Michael

O'Reilly might smash his fist into the face of Joe S. Hardee? Michael had sworn to do just that any number of times during his stay in Stalag Luft I. Each time a member of his squadron arrived in camp—those who would have known Hardee—Michael would question him about the fate of Hardee. Was he still flying? Did he finish his tour, or had he, too, been shot down? Was he alive or dead? What had happened to him when he had returned to base after that mission on which Michael and his crew were shot out of the sky over Germany? All Michael ever knew for certain was that Joe S. Hardee finished his tour and was sent back to the States as a major. He had heard that Hardee was reprimanded by the squadron commander, but he had never met anyone who knew for certain that had happened.

"Christ!" Michael said. "I should never have come." He changed from business suit to sport jacket and slacks and went down to the lobby. He entered the Esplanade, where the reunion registration booths were set up. Two men were hanging prints of aircraft drawings in a display room off the Esplanade. Another man was setting up a table with jewelry emblazoned with the Eighth Air Force emblem. Michael thought he might look at them later, if he stayed. A stylish looking woman came into the Esplanade and went behind one of the registration desks. She looked familiar to Michael. He watched her.

She was undoubtedly in her fifties. But she had the figure and the carriage of a much younger woman. He squinted his eyes and tried to imagine her with a darker tone in her hair and a fresher look to her face.

Emily. Emily Gates. The Red Cross girl attached to the 612th. He was certain of it. He crossed to the booth and watched her pin on her name tag. When it was in place, he took out his glasses and peered at it. "Emily Tornquist," it read. The woman smiled at him.

"Emily Gates," Michael said.

"Right!" the woman said. And the light of recognition lit up her eyes.

"I'm Mike O'Reilly," Michael said.

"Oh, my God," Emily said. She swept out from behind the booth and took Michael's hands. "Oh, God! Mike! I can't believe it! You were listed K.I.A. I never heard anything to the contrary. Oh, my God! I thought you were dead!" She began to cry but quickly caught herself. "Thirty-five years! It's a miracle!"

Michael was stunned into speechlessness by her greeting. He and Emily had been friends. They had shared common friends among the English civilians who frequented The Cricketers, the small pub on an out-of-the-way road on the edge of Bedford. But they had never been intimate. It was Tommy Nash, his copilot, who had, against all the odds, captured the most beautiful Gray Lady in the First Air Division. Of all the thousands of officers, from brigadier general down to second lieutenant, who had taken a run at Emily, it was the slender, quiet student from California, Tommy Nash, who had, without trying, been loved by Emily. For the five frantic months they had been with the group, Emily and Tommy had been lovers and it was assumed that when Tommy finished his tour, he and Emily would marry.

Emily turned off the overhead light in the booth and gathered up her paraphernalia.

"I'm early," she said. "Let's go someplace quiet. I want to know what happened. I have to know."

At a corner table in the coffee shop, Michael told Emily about that final bombing mission. He remembered it with a clarity and detail that surprised him. Emily had been there at the hardstand before takeoff. But as Michael told his narrative, he spoke as if she had not been. She kept silent during it all. At the first mention of Tommy Nash's name, there had been a look of pain in her eyes, which Michael caught. He decided then not to tell her the exact circumstances of Tommy's death.

The target had been Braunschweig in central Germany. Michael had been there before and knew it for a target that the Luftwaffe would defend ferociously.

It would also be the final mission for Michael and his crew, their twenty-fifth. It had been the custom to allow a crew commander the option of choosing what target he would fly against on his final mission, and many waited for a short hop across the English Channel to hit a target in France. There was no guarantee that in France the enemy opposition would be negligible. But the time was March 1944, and since October of 1943, the air offensive against Germany and "Fortress Europe" had mounted in size and intensity, and the Luftwaffe especially had sustained terrible losses. Intelligence reports indicated that the Germans would send up the Luftwaffe in great numbers only when the bombers entered German airspace. So, the French and Belgian targets were considered to be fairly easy ones.

Michael had asked the crew how they felt about Braunschweig. His own feeling had been that one target on any day was as dangerous as another. They had agreed. So, they went along, and Michael had chosen to fly lead of the second element in the high squadron, a position in the formation only a little less vulnerable to fighter attack.

Despite the target, the mood among the crew was one of high optimism. They had survived the worst of the air battles—the first Schweinfurt–Halberstadt on January 11, Big Week in February, and the first three Berlin raids. In that time, they had been shot up but not down. Only one crewman had been lost, and he had been a replacement for the tail gunner, Sid Levy, who had missed a mission because of an infected tooth. The crew had remained intact and unscathed through twenty-four missions, and every man felt invincible.

Even Tommy Nash, the poet-philosopher, the pacifist by conviction who had enlisted because of a moral compulsion to fight against Nazism, had broken out of his usual shell of pre-takeoff silence. By dusk that same day, he would be free of his commitment to fly one complete tour of duty before he could request a transfer to noncombatant status. He should have left Michael's crew and been assigned an aircraft and crew of his own as first pilot. He had refused the opportunity. It would have meant the responsibility for nine other lives and a more direct participation in the planning of bombing raids, raids that would kill people. He had been able to accept the rationalization that his role as a copilot was a passive one, related only to the operation of the aircraft.

The 612th had reached Braunschweig twenty minutes after the first group of B-17s had unloaded and turned off. Even that provided an extra margin of safety. The lead group would absorb initial fighter attacks and, as it passed over the target, would drop millions of strips of aluminized paper called "chaff," which would play absolute hell with ground artillery radar.

As it happened, the route into Braunschweig was as free of enemy harassment as a training mission back in the States. The flak over the target was scattered and ineffectual, at least a thousand feet beneath the formations. The bomb run was a little too leisurely for Michael's comfort. But it was completed without damage from the still ineffectual flak.

If Michael had had any misgivings about the mission at all, it was the fact that the route homeward was the exact reverse of the route in. The route was as straight as an arrow. There had been no fighter interception on the way to the target. But the lead group had already begun its homeward journey. The German fighter controller could gamble that the other groups would follow.

Another doubtful element turned out to be Captain Joe S. Hardee, who had been chosen to fly the lead aircraft in the high squadron. His leadership on the way to the target had been sloppy. The high squadron had drifted out from the lead squadron a number of times. Michael could imagine Hardee's copilot nudging Hardee—who took advice and correction badly—to get back into position, to keep the formation tight. But when Hardee made the move, it was sudden and too strong. The pilot flying on Hardee's left wing had to throttle back to avoid either over-running the formation or colliding with Hardee. The pilot on the right wing had to ram his throttles full forward to keep up. As lead of the second element, Michael did his best to minimize the effect of Hardee's almost violent maneuver on the aircraft flying off his wings. He had had to lag too far behind several times. Luckily, there were no Luftwaffe fighters in the area then.

The way home had been a different story. Halfway to the Dutch coast, Hardee had again allowed the high squadron to drift out, this time more than a half mile. Perhaps he had been lulled by the serenity of the skies over Germany so far. Lieutenant Harvey Olsen, who was flying in the box, the seventh position in the high squadron directly behind and above Michael, apparently had been worried. He left his slot as if he intended to cross the open space and tack onto the lead squadron for protection.

The Luftwaffe came in with the afternoon sun behind them. There was no warning, no calls over the command channel that bandits were in the area. Nor was there any sign of friendly escort.

"Fighters! Bounce!" Michael heard on the intercom. It must have been Raeburn, the bombardier. Michael hauled back on the control column. He had not seen the fighters and did not know until later that they were FW-190s, eight of them. But already it was too late. He heard the sharp crack of an exploding twenty-millimeter cannon shell. He turned slightly to his right and saw that Tommy Nash had been slammed back against his seat. Half his head had been shot away.

"I'm hit! I'm hit!" someone else shouted on the intercom.

"They got Olsen!" came another shout. "Jesus—he exploded!"

Michael's aircraft suddenly fell off on the left wing. He struggled to bring it back to level flight. There was no hope of help from Nash, who was very obviously dead. The flight deck had suddenly filled with acrid smoke and tiny particles of debris. Michael could smell the smoke through his oxygen mask. Several of the gunners were trying to use the intercom at the same time. Michael feathered the propeller of the outside port engine and fought the airplane back to level flight.

"At ease!" he shouted. There was immediate silence except for the heavy hammering of fifty-caliber machine guns.

"Got the son of a bitch!"

"Six o'clock high!" More hammering. "Jesus, skipper, hold the fucking thing straight!"

The Fortress had dropped out of the formation. Michael increased power on the three good engines and tried to catch up. "Here they come!" There was another explosion and then another. The inner port engine trailed white smoke.

"Fire!" came a shout. "The bomb bay's fulla fire!"

There was a layer of clouds thousands of feet below. Michael shoved the control column forward. There was no escape. The best he could hope for was the protection of the clouds until the escort fighters showed up.

The hammering of the fifty-caliber guns had been continuous. Michael had seen the attacking fighters only once, dead ahead, two of them turning in for a head-on pass. He saw one emit a small trail of black smoke, then explode. The other broke off. There was the sharp crack again of twenty-millimeter bursts. The center of the instrument panel disappeared. The inboard starboard engine exploded. Michael punched the bail-out signal and hauled back on the control column. He would hold the airplane straight and level as long as he could.

"Kolchick's had it!" the bombardier said. Michael engaged the automatic pilot and hoped to God it would work. He left his seat and saw his engineer and top-turret gunner, Minetti, struggling to hook his parachute pack onto his harness. Minetti's oxygen mask was still hooked up. Michael disengaged it and slapped him on the leg. Minetti looked at him with frightened eyes and then pushed past him and clambered toward the escape hatch below the flight deck. Michael saw Raeburn, the bombardier, slip through the forward hatch.

Michael had not heard from the five crewmen in the rear of the aircraft—Jordan, the radio operator, the waist gunners, Gilson and

McKinney, Moulton, the ball turret gunner, or tail gunner Levy.

He grabbed his parachute pack and struggled into the bomb bay. The fire was out but he had been able to see the ground below and the entire right wing of the plane through an enormous hole in the fuselage. He bucked himself between the bomb-rack stanchions and gained the radio room. It was a shambles. Jordan was just disappearing through the rear door of the room. Michael followed him and saw him shove past the two waist gunners and dive through the rear escape hatch.

Gilson, the left waist gunner, was supporting McKinney, who was conscious but injured. Michael helped him dump McKinney through the hatch. Then Gilson went. Michael tried to look past the tail wheel still tucked in the fuselage to see if Levy had gotten out.

Suddenly, he felt an incredible force compressing him. He lost consciousness, or thought he had. The next thing he could recall was tumbling through the air amidst a cloud of debris. There was no sound, no sound at all. Not even of air rushing. He realized that he was falling earthward at a great rate. He reached for the D-ring on his parachute pack and muttered a "thank God" that it was there. He pulled it. The small pilot chute popped out, hauling the main chute, twenty-eight feet in diameter, after it. Michael had expected a tremendous jerk when the chute opened. Instead, there was a mild jarring, a barely audible "pop!" as the canopy filled, and then he was swinging in the harness and falling gently. He counted seven parachutes below him. That meant Levy had made it.

He saw nothing of his aircraft. Then he heard the steady drone of the Eighth Air Force driving on toward England, and he was conscious of a roaring anger. A Focke Wulf 190 flew past him. But his anger was directed at his comrades who were deserting him and at the stupid, incompetent bastard Hardee.

They were all captured within an hour after touching down. They had landed in a farming area where there was not the slightest cover. Soldiers and civilians had converged on them, and for a brief time, there was a dispute between the civilians and the soldiers about hanging "den Luftgängen," "die Terrorflieger." Fortunately, the soldiers won the debate.

Later, at the home airbase of the Luftwaffe fighters that shot down Michael's B-17 and Olsen's, Michael was shown the bodies of Nash and Kolchick. He was told that there were two survivors from the "other" bomber, presumably Olsen's. In the interrogation center at Obereussel, near Frankfurt, more than a week later, Michael met Sergeant Jerry Rasmussen, Olsen's flight engineer. They both had vowed then, and they meant it, that Hardee would pay for the deaths of their friends. Michael swore to smash Hardee's face in. Rasmussen would settle for nothing less than death.

Michael did not tell Emily all of this, although as he talked and selected his words, all of it passed through his mind like a motion picture. He smelled the stench of battle and heard the noises. He felt again the damp cold of that March afternoon, and in the comfortable atmosphere of the Wardman Park coffee shop, his body was clammy with the sweat of a remembered fear.

"What a sweet boy Tommy was," Emily said softly. "I think we would have married. He wrote his parents about me, and I went to see them after I got home from England." She lit a cigarette. "I was terribly broken up, you know. You were all reported killed. I was sent home because I committed the cardinal sin for a Red Cross lady. I fell in love with a soldier." She touched his hand. "I'm so happy most of you survived. This is my third reunion. I didn't make the first one. I see more and more faces that used to be so familiar. I wonder why I keep coming back. Vanity—I suppose. I like to be reassured that I haven't aged as much as everyone else."

"You haven't," Michael said. He meant it.

Emily smiled. "You're a dear," she said. "You know—now that I think of it—I come to these reunions to see how people turned out. The ones I knew fairly well, I mean." She shook her head. "Some of it is very sad."

"Winners and losers?" Michael asked.

"Yes," Emily said. "Someone you thought would skyrocket to the top. Well—a fizzle. And the squadron dope turns out to be a corporation lawyer."

"What about you?" Michael asked.

"A little bit of both," Emily said. "I have my own cosmetics business back in Kentucky. But—I'm divorced. I have two grown children. I'm a happy grandmother three times. But I live alone. I know a great many people in a lot of different places. But I have no friends. I live a very busy life. But it's not an exciting one or a particularly useful one." She closed her eyes and tossed her head. "My God, how I wallow in self-pity. I'm sorry, Mike." She laughed. "Remember how I used to cry on your shoulder, worrying about Tommy?"

"Big brother," Michael said, and smiled at the memory. "I used to get so goddamn mad. I was trying to make out with Sylvia What's-Her-Name, and you would have me off in a corner of The Cricketers, crying in my beer. You loused up a lot of dates for me."

"I kept you pure," Emily said. "Or reasonably so."

"I didn't want to be pure," Michael said. "You know nothing counts in wartime. The combat soldier has a free pass."

"An interesting theological concept," Emily said.

"I got that from Tommy," Michael said.

They were both silent for a bit.

"It sounds crazy," Emily said, "but they were *good* days."

"Best war we ever had," Michael said. "Maybe that's why we come to these things. Makes us feel noble as hell. I remember reading once about a reunion of knights who fought in the Crusades. It was something like twenty years later. People scoffed at them. But they ignored that. They came together for themselves. To celebrate what they once were."

"We did do a fine thing," Emily said. "Didn't we? I mean all of us. Red Cross girls like me. Even if it was a lark for some. Even the worst of us was doing something worthwhile."

"General absolution," Michael said. He was thinking of Joe S.

Hardee. Emily did not understand.

"You've lost me, Mike," she said.

"When the war is over, we will all be friends again," he said. "Forgive and forget. Like with the Germans."

"It must have been incredibly hard," Emily said, perhaps understanding now.

"It still is," Michael replied.

Again, Emily touched his hand.

They talked a little more. He told her about Chrissie and their four children and the family business and showed her pictures of his grandchildren. And then it was time for her to return to the registration area. She refused Michael's offer to walk with her.

"Finish your coffee," she said. "I'll see you in the group hospitality room. It opens at three o'clock." Then she left, walking with a fluid grace. Michael visualized her in her gray flannel suit and the peaked cap and her cool, controlled manner and remembered how he had put her down at first for a snotty Southern aristocrat.

Michael left the coffee shop and went to the lobby. It was more crowded now, as was the Esplanade. There were a number of men about his own age with attractive wives with bright, inquiring faces. Some of them wore tags with their names and their unit designation on them. The unit numbers were large enough to be seen without squinting. He saw no "612" tags. Since he wore no tag, he was ignored.

He reentered the Esplanade, still uncertain whether to participate in the reunion beyond hanging about the lobby and dropping in at least for a quick look-see at the hospitality room. He found himself scrutinizing faces. He saw none that even ticked his memory.

Emily was not at the registration booth. A young woman, perhaps in her mid-twenties, was there instead. Michael walked up to her station. She was wearing a 612th tag. She noticed his puzzlement.

"My father was in the 612th," she said. "Are you registered?"

"No," he said. He was irritated by his own indecision. "I'm in Washington on other business," he lied. "I saw all the signs in the lobby and I was thinking of staying around. Can I register later on? I'm already staying at the hotel."

"Oh, certainly," the young lady said. She gathered up several pieces of printed material. "The only problem might be the big dinner tomorrow night. We have only so many places. We would have to know before tomorrow afternoon. That's when the bulk of the people will get here."

Michael thanked her and assured her he would make up his mind long before the deadline. He went into the bar, ordered a scotch, and examined the material the girl had given him. The only thing of interest was a sheet with the names of those who had registered by mail. The names were grouped by units. He looked over the list, which was rather large, of those who had been with the 612th.

There were not many familiar names. No first names, only initials. There was no rank or squadron designation or differentiation between ground personnel and aircrew. There was no listing for a Hardee or a J. Rasmussen. None of his own crew were on the list. He would have been surprised if any had been. There had been little or no correspondence among them that he knew of since the war.

Several men came into the bar. All were tagged, and all were in good spirits. They all glanced in Michael's direction, saw that he wore no tag, and lost interest. That annoyed Michael.

He finished his drink, paid the bartender, and strode from the bar. He went directly to the Esplanade to the booth where the same young lady he had spoken to earlier was still sitting.

"I want to sign up," he said. "For everything—lunches, sight-seeing, the Saturday night dinner, the works."

"Do you want to join the society, too?" she asked. He looked at a sign behind her, on which was emblazoned the insignia of the Eighth Air Force encircled by a white band with the words "The Eighth Air Force Historical Society."

"Yes," he said, "I think I do."

He filled out the necessary forms and handed them back to the girl with payment of his dues for the society, the registration fee, and the cost of the various events. The girl seemed pleased that he, too, had been with the 612th.

"When were you with the group?" she asked.

He told her.

"Oh—you must have been one of the old-timers," she said. "My father didn't get to the 612th until after D-Day."

He affixed the tag to his lapel and felt self-conscious. He had never liked them. If someone wanted to know who he was, why, they could simply ask. He did recognize a certain usefulness. They helped to sort out who belonged to what among the hundreds who were in the hotel for various conventions, meetings, and so forth. But that was only alright if one did not mind being accosted every ten steps by total strangers who seemed to believe that a tag similar to theirs entitled them to instant intimacy with the wearer.

Nothing of the sort happened to Michael as he crossed the lobby again toward the bar. There were a few who nodded and smiled pleasantly. He did not encounter anyone from the 612th. He would have a drink, he thought, and then see if Emily might join him for lunch. If she returned to the Esplanade.

Michael ordered another scotch and brought it to a table near a window that looked out on what had once been the hotel's center court and garden. It was ugly with the skeleton of the new building and the clutter of construction.

An older man dressed in an expensive-looking camel's hair sports jacket and slacks came over. He was wearing a 612th tag.

"Mind if I join you?" he asked.

"Of course not," Michael said. The man placed his drink on the table and stuck out his hand. Michael took it.

"Chip Collins," the man said, and instantly Michael recognized the brittle gray eyes and easy smile of Major Chip Collins, squadron flight operations and executive officer.

"Mike O'Reilly," he said. They laughed together.

"Never would have known you," Collins said. "You're packing a little more weight and less hair, and those eyeglasses hide a lot."

"You don't look as if you've been packed in ice for thirty-five years," Mike said. He had been especially fond of Collins then, despite the difference in their ages and their ranks. Collins was the pilot who had checked Michael out and declared his crew to be fit and ready for combat. He had been a teacher in Indiana, and a more unlikely teacher Mike could not imagine. "You still teaching?" Michael asked.

"Hell no," Chip said. "I own a cow farm and a chain of overpriced restaurants in Kansas. I'm half-retired and I play a lot of golf and do a lot of hunting to keep from going crazy. How about you? I never did know what you did when there wasn't any war."

"Towing," Michael said. "Harbor towing. Tugs. We do some open water work, too. Family business."

"Now, that's one thing I would like to own, a goddamn tugboat!" Collins said. "It'd look kinda funny out in Kansas, even with wheels on." He laughed heartily at the idea. He raised his glass. "Here's how!" He tossed his drink down, sat back, and folded his hands across his stomach. "I really look forward to these reunions, Mike. I belong to every goddamn organization chartered in the state of Kansas, but this is the only one I give a damn about. Went to England with the group last year and saw the old base. It's still active, you know. Royal Air Force. It's a huge experimental station. Nothing left of the old place except a couple of Nissen huts and the old officers' B mess, which is a storehouse. But it was great. Bedford's changed. But there were a couple of familiar places: The Silver Grille, The Swan, The King's Arms and The Cricketers."

"That was my favorite, The Cricketers," Michael said. "Mr. and Mrs. Doug were going to throw a party for me and my crew. But—" He left the sentence unfinished. "They put two bottles of scotch away. And you know how hard it was for them to get the scotch. I wonder what happened to them."

"The way the English are, they're probably still there," Collins said. He got up to get himself another drink. Michael declined another. He watched Collins walk—swagger, really—to the bar. It was difficult to visualize him in a leather flight jacket, slender and broad-shouldered with a mop of unruly red hair. Collins had been a good, serious pilot and a fine officer—on the base. In London, on forty-eight-hour leave, he was a wild man. "Fight hard. Play hard. You're only on the track one time." That was Collins's philosophy.

Collins fell into conversation with another man at the bar.

He brought him over.

"We'll make this table 612th operations," Collins said. "You oughta remember Al Daniels. He started out with Heywood and checked out right after Halberstadt." Michael did remember Daniels, a tall, baby-faced kid who had been a star athlete at Syracuse. He had captained the 369th Squadron basketball team. Olsen had been a member of it. Michael shook his hand.

"I wondered what happened to you," Daniels said. "We heard you exploded."

Michael decided to explain what had happened, more briefly than he did for Emily but more technically. It was as if he were being debriefed after the mission. He felt an immediacy about the moment that caused a tension inside himself. The two men opposite him were leaning forward. Their faces grew grave, attentive. When Michael told them about Olsen having to leave the high squadron to find safety in the lead squadron, Collins swore. Daniels shook his head. They were silent when Michael finished.

"Did you know that you and Olsen were the only two lost that day to enemy fighters?" Collins asked.

Michael shrugged. "That doesn't change things, does it?" he said. "It's strange—going over all this thirty-five years after the fact. But I'm just as mad now as I was then."

"Rip Ryan grounded him," Collins said. "Wouldn't let him fly with the squadron after that. Finally got rid of him. I don't know where he went."

"Hardee?" Michael asked.

"Who else?" Collins said. "Tyler was his copilot. He raised holy hell when they got on the ground. Took a poke at Hardee at the club that night. Christ! I'd forgotten that. I was with the group from the beginning to the goddamn end, and I must have dealt with hundreds of crews. Hundreds. And there's damn few I remember. But I remember you and Olsen and Daniels here like it was yesterday, now that my memory's jerked."

It was Daniels who posed out loud the question that Michael realized he had been trying to avoid. "What would you do if Hardee walked in here right now?" he said.

"I don't know," Michael said. "Probably nothing. I haven't been in a fistfight since my twenties. It would look pretty ridiculous for two middle-aged men to be scuffling around a bar room."

"You're right," Collins said. "Still—"

"He hasn't shown up so far," Daniels said. "And this is my fourth reunion."

"What about Rasmussen?" Michael asked. "He swore he'd kill Hardee. Olsen was a god to Rasmussen."

"No," Daniels said. "He hasn't come either. But that's not unusual. I've been involved in the group track-down operation. You know—trying to locate former members and then trying to get them to join. After thirty years, people get lost. They retire. They die. They couldn't care less. The addresses we get from old records are out-of-date by years and years. I'm surprised we have as big a membership as we have. And you have to have the time and money to make a reunion. A lot of guys are retired and can take the time. But a hell of a lot more are still working, and they're not about to spend their vacations at a reunion."

"Forget Hardee," Collins said. "Enjoy yourself. There's a film show this afternoon. A lot of old combat footage. I'm gonna go and shit my pants again for old times' sake."

They separated, and Michael had lunch by himself. He felt relieved. He had finally been able to tell someone who had been a part of his military life what had happened and how he felt. It was as if he had given his final report. The mission was completed and the case closed. He could now consign Hardee to the outer darkness.

He attended the film showing and understood what Collins had been talking about. The film was in color and its clarity was surprisingly good, considering it was made in 1943. The cameraman knew what to aim his camera at. It was not a film for the squeamish. Michael was drawn into the mission the film depicted as surely as if he were actually flying it. And he knew that he was not the only one in the audience who felt that way. The flak, those greasy, ominous puffs of black smoke that appeared without sound, caused his stomach muscles to tighten. Whoever made the film did not trick it up with phony sound effects. All one heard was the incessant hammering of the machine guns and the constant drone of engines. The chatter over the intercom was real. Michael actually flinched when enemy fighters suddenly appeared. And he grunted with satisfaction when one exploded.

On the way out of the viewing room, Michael thought of Chrissie. He would have liked her to have seen the film. There were quite a few wives in the room, and he saw the looks of wonderment on their faces. He heard one gentle-looking woman say to her equally gentle-looking husband: "That's what it was like. You never said."

Michael looked at his watch. Right now, Chrissie would be at the hospital, where she was a volunteer therapist. He would call her at about five and urge her to come down to Washington. He felt ill at ease without her. He wanted her to share the experience with him. It seemed like Hardee was out of his system. He was somewhat startled to realize that he had been worried about a confrontation. Now he could relax and immerse himself in the waters of nostalgia. Be sentimental and think good thoughts, Emily had said earlier. Well, why not? He was, after all, one of a company of heroes. He had fought a kind of warfare that would never be seen again. Bombers in formation driving relentlessly, invincibly, against a formidable and daring enemy. And never turning back in the face of the enemy. Not once. A company of heroes. He liked that idea.

He went up to the fourth floor of the Wardman Tower, but the hospitality room was not yet open. He checked at the registration desk and learned that it would not be open until the following day, when two of the officers of the 612th group committee arrived. That left the afternoon to kill until the cocktail reception for early arrivals. He went to his suite and called Chrissie.

"I'd like you to come down to Washington," he told her. "I think you'll enjoy it." He went over the program of events with her. "We've never done the sightseeing tour thing, as often as we've been to Washington."

"Are you alright?" was her response. It was the kind of question Chrissie would always ask when he suggested something that was out of the ordinary for them. Like the time he wanted to attend a Benny Goodman concert in Central Park. She thought he was getting dotty. They had not done that kind of thing for twenty years. Going out was not something you did on the spur of the moment. There had to be a reason. Things like that had to fit into an orderly and predictable routine.

"Of course I'm alright," he told her. "Why does something have to be wrong when I ask you to do something like this? Throw some things into a bag and come down."

"You know I can't just run off like that, Mike," Chrissie said. "I wish you had suggested this earlier."

"Never mind," he said. "I just thought it would be nice to be together for a weekend. Just the two of us." He wanted to shout at her, to tell her to go to hell. Instead, he made another attempt. "Think about it, and I'll call you again tonight." She agreed to think about it, but she sounded as if she would decide against joining him. He felt defeated and deflated. He lay back on his bed and looked at the ceiling. He closed his eyes, and scenes from the film he had seen earlier flashed across his mind. He heard the guns and the roar of the engines again. The telephone rang, and the screen went black. He sat up and picked up the instrument. It was Emily.

"How about a drink, Mike?" she said. "I'm free for a while."

"You have a deal," he said. He wondered as he hung up if he was doing the right thing. Emily was a most attractive woman. And the suggestion that their meeting might extend beyond the time spent with a couple of cocktails was definitely there.

Well, it wouldn't be the first time he had strayed from marital fidelity, although it had been a long time since the last episode. A very long time. He knocked his knuckles against his forehead. Incredible! *I'm in some kind of crazy time warp*, he thought. *This is not 1944, and Emily and I are not in our twenties. What the hell am I thinking of?*

Yet he was aware of a surge of excitement as he showered and shaved and dressed in a navy blue blazer and gray slacks. He admitted that he looked pretty trim and youthful for a man of fifty-seven.

Emily looked spectacular for a woman at least as old as Michael. She wore a simple black cocktail dress with very little ornament, the most prominent being her name tag. Michael had forgotten his. She brought him into the Esplanade and got him another one.

They ran into Collins and Daniels in the bar, and for an hour or so, the war stories flew thick and fast. Michael could not remember when he had enjoyed himself more. Then Collins and Daniels drifted off. They were on their way to Georgetown, where they had heard the action was.

"They might as well play tonight," Emily said. "Their families will be in tomorrow." There was no hint of reproval in her voice.

"Might as well go the distance," Mike said. "How about dinner?" Emily looked at her watch.

"We just about have enough time," she said. "General Doolittle is coming in for the reception, and I'm on the welcoming committee. Do you mind? I wish we could just fly away from here and—" She looked away. "You're a very attractive man, Mike. And you've changed a great deal."

"You are a beautiful woman, Emily," Mike said. "I'm flattered to be with you. But you're my friend, too. I don't want to even bruise that friendship."

Emily nodded and smiled. "Let's sweep into the dining room and dazzle the hell out of everybody," she said.

The dinner went quickly and pleasantly, and Emily left Michael to go to her room to change for the reception. He was alone again. He went back to the lobby, which was now teeming with people. There were mostly men in black tie with women in evening gowns. A few military uniforms were in evidence, and the Eighth Air Force contingent was most noticeable for the ever-present name tag and the range of dress from black tie to ranch suits and string tie.

There was a commotion at the main entrance, and Michael stopped to see what was happening. He recognized the small bald man in his late seventies who came in. General Jimmy Doolittle, aviation pioneer, air racer, the hero of the Tokyo raid, and commanding general of the Eighth Air Force after Ira Eaker.

Doolittle was surrounded immediately. Michael did not have much more than historical interest in Doolittle. His combat service had been under Eaker and Spaatz. As far as he was concerned, Doolittle was a latecomer. So, he left the lobby and went into the exhibition room off the Esplanade and looked at the display of aircraft models, photographs, aviation art, and memorabilia on display.

There he met two more 612th veterans: Neftziger, a bombardier, and Tolan, a navigator. They, too, were surprised that he was alive and well. And he was surprised that they would remember.

"Hell," Tolan said. "It caused a stink. But the son of a bitch got off easy, as far as I heard."

"Water over the dam," Michael said. They moved to a table on which was displayed a volume covered in blue leather with the Eighth Air Force insignia embossed on it in gold. Michael picked it up and thumbed through it. It was a collection of photographs of the Eighth Air Force in action. He checked the index for references to the 612th. There was a large number of them. He, Tolan, and Neftziger looked at the photographs together, pointing out familiar faces or aircraft when the markings could be seen. Michael stopped at a page with a photograph of the operations staff of the 369th Squadron. He saw himself behind Collins, barely recognizable. He had no recollection of the photograph being taken. The group was standing outside squadron operations near the flight line. At the far right of the picture, three places removed from the squadron commander, Lieutenant Colonel "Rip" Ryan, stood Captain Joe S. Hardee. He was a short, stocky man with a wide face and a pencil-thin mustache. He stood out clearly. Michael checked the list of names below the photograph. Hardee was listed. It was him.

Michael put the book on the table. His hands had begun to shake, and he felt a fresh surge of anger, of hatred. He excused himself to Tolan and Neftziger and walked rapidly from the room. He hurried through the lobby and out into the cool night. He felt nauseous. He gulped in the fresh air and felt his anger begin to abate. His hands stopped shaking. But his face was covered with a fine film of sweat.

"Jesus Christ Almighty!" he muttered. "I hate that rotten bastard!" He headed down the driveway to the street. He left the hotel grounds and walked to Connecticut Avenue, turning north. He had to deal with this hatred, this rage. It was as strong and as consuming as the day he had been shot down. Why? Was it the death of ten men, especially Tommy Nash and Stan Kolchick? God! He only knew three or four of them by name. Was it the fourteen months in prison camp? In retrospect, it wasn't that bad. It was an officers' camp, and the Germans, except for a couple of occasions, had been at least correct in their treatment of the prisoners of war. Something was eluding him.

But there *had* been something he heard long ago that increased his anger at Hardee geometrically. What the hell had it been? Then he remembered—Don Renz. Don Renz, who had been right behind Michael in seniority, in efficiency rating, in promise. Michael was to have returned home for thirty days when his tour was over and then return to the squadron. By that time, he would have been a major and in line for squadron commander. If he had lasted out the European war and then the war against Japan, he would have made at least colonel. But his "tour" played out in Stalag Luft I. At twenty-five years of age, Don Renz had been promoted to full colonel in the United States Army Air Force when it should have been Michael O'Reilly.

And Michael O'Reilly would have more than satisfied the ambition of his father, who had been a captain of cavalry in the First World War and who had retired from the Army Reserves as a brigadier general. He would also have eclipsed his brother, Terence, who had earned the rank of lieutenant colonel as an infantry officer both in World War II and in Korea, where he died in action. Michael had been a reserve major, which did not count with his father. Active duty rank only was the standard. And the highest active duty rank Michael had held was first lieutenant, even if he was promoted to captain just prior to his discharge. The only palliative to his father's disappointment was Michael's decorations. Not even Terence could claim the Silver Star and the Distinguished Flying Cross with two Oak Leaf Clusters. On the other hand, Michael had also been taken prisoner. That, too, did not sit well with his father, although the circumstances of having been taken "behind enemy lines" was preferable to having been taken in the midst of battle.

No, Michael told himself, he could not use Renz or his father to explain the wracking storm of hate and anger that had erupted so suddenly and so violently. He was angry for *himself*. He, Michael O'Reilly, had suffered at the hands of Captain Joe S. Hardee. Tommy Nash had no ambition but to live his life out in peace. Did Kolchick? Michael had never known much about Kolchick. He and Tommy were dead, and there was no point in speculating.

Michael's thoughts shocked him. Was he that shallow? Or was

he indulging again in his old game of finding fault with himself before he would find fault with others? God knows, he had done too much of that after the war. A friend had told him that he suffered from "uniformitis," an affliction in which the victim believed that his authority sprang only from the insignia of rank and the uniform of authority. Once out of it, the victim lost all self-confidence. It had taken years of agonizing effort on Michael's part to probe and discover his own resources and to then use them. He had done it alone and in secret. Not even Chrissie had known how desperate he had been. But he ran the family business now with a strong and sure hand and had come to be regarded as one of the toughest men in the business. Now Hardee had surfaced, and Michael felt himself again in danger of being shot down.

Goddammit! he thought. He had to get Hardee out of his system once and for all. Yet he did not know how that could be done if Hardee did not appear at this reunion. If he did not, Michael knew that he would never again attend an Eighth Air Force reunion and that he might very well lose all that he had gained.

When he stopped walking, Michael had no idea where he was. He was tired. He flagged down a taxi and directed the driver to the hotel. He was surprised to see how far he had walked.

The cocktail party was in full swing. The huge Park Room was jammed, and the four portable bars were all three deep. Michael squeezed up to one of them and got himself a scotch. He moved back against a wall to stay out of the press of people and to observe. He felt surprisingly calm and collected. He had gotten hold of himself on the taxi ride back from his walk and decided that he had been on a brief emotional binge. It had been a time warp. He had been back in 1944. It must have been the drinks and the reliving, first with Emily and then with Collins and Daniels, of those shattering last moments of his last mission. It was thirty-five years into the present now, and he was the man who had arrived in Washington that morning fully in control of his life. He knew again who he was.

Emily appeared. She was wearing a long deep-red gown that was stunning in its effect.

"Mike, I've been looking all over for you," she said. "Did you meet the general?"

"No," he answered.

"Too bad," Emily said. "He left a few minutes ago."

Michael felt relieved. He did not want to tell Emily that he had no interest in General Doolittle.

Collins joined them. "Georgetown was a washout," he said. "No place for an old codger like me. Jack Siefert showed up, and the hospitality suite will be open in a half hour. There are about thirty, forty guys from the 612th here, and we're all going to blow this nuthouse and hold a rump reunion in the suite."

"Count me in," Michael said. He looked at Emily.

"Yes," she said. "After all, the 612th was my group, too."

Michael checked at the front desk to see if Chrissie had called back. She hadn't. He debated whether to call her then or wait until later. He decided to wait until eleven, an hour from then.

There were half a dozen people waiting at the tower elevator. Only two, a man and a woman, did not wear name tags. They regarded the others with curiosity.

"All Eighth Air Force?" the man asked. He spoke with an accent.

"Right," someone answered.

"I am Dutch," the man said. "I used to watch you come over almost every day. What a magnificent sight! We used to cheer until the Nazis forbade it. One could be shot for cheering."

The elevator arrived and filled immediately. At the fourth floor, it emptied out again, except for the couple from Holland. As Michael departed, the man smiled and waved at him and said, "Goodnight and good luck."

The hospitality suite consisted of a large sitting room and two bedrooms, one on each side. Immediately inside to the right was the "bar," a long table covered with a white cloth on which was an array of liquor and mixers. An ice bucket serving as a "kitty" was already overflowing with dollar bills. On the left was another table holding an enormous model of a B-17 with electrically operated propellers. It looked real. The sitting room was packed with people, men and women whom Michael had not seen before.

Daniels caught Michael at the door.

"Would you believe Rasmussen's here?" he asked. "He was looking for you. He's feeling pretty good."

Michael followed Daniels into the room. Emily had already gone in. They both understood that there could be no hint of their being "together." She was still the "Red Cross Lady" who was friend to all—equally.

Rasmussen was talking to a group near the window that opened onto a small terrace. The group was laughing loudly. Rasmussen had changed hardly at all. His hair was still a deep chestnut and his face lean and smooth. His body was still spare. His clothes seemed overlarge and well-worn. He recognized Michael and smiled. But Michael noticed right away that Rasmussen's almost purple eyes showed no humor, no warmth.

They shook hands. "Been a long, long time," Rasmussen said. "You look like life treated you pretty good."

"It has," Michael said.

"I only live a little ways from here in West Virginia," Rasmussen said. "That's the only way I could make it."

"It's good to see you, Ras," Michael said.

"It's good to see you!" Rasmussen said. Then after a pause, "Can I talk to you?" He indicated the terrace. Michael followed him out.

"Look—I don't wanna call you lieutenant or captain or what ever you finally made," Rasmussen said.

"Call me Mike," Michael said. "That's my name, and we're not in the Army anymore."

Rasmussen seemed relieved. "Jesus, Mike," he said. "This is the first time in my life I've ever been in a place like this. I don't know how to act."

"Come on, Ras," Michael said. "Be yourself. Everybody's the

same here. The war is over."

"Right," Rasmussen said. He took a swallow from his drink. "Mike," he said, "I come here hoping I'd catch up with Hardee."

"Ras," Michael said quickly, "the bastard isn't worth it."

"No, no, Mike," Rasmussen said. "I wouldn't do nothing. I just want to look at that no-good prick and see if he can look me in the goddamn eye. I want to do that in front of everyone."

"I don't think he'll be here, Ras," Michael said. "He hasn't been to one yet. He could be dead, for all we know. I don't care. I don't want any part of him. It's all over."

"No, no!" Rasmussen said. He grasped Michael's arm in a grip that hurt and leaned his face close to Michael's, his breath sharp with alcohol. "He's *here*! In Washington! In the goddamn *Pentagon*! He's a buck-fuckin' general! A *general*!" He paused to let the news sink in.

"Hardee? I don't believe it!" Michael said.

"True!" Rasmussen said. "I read it in *Air Force Times*. I get it regular in the mail. I seen it myself. Brigadier General Joe S. Hardee, U.S.A.F. He's a procurement officer. And he's going to be here because he's going to be at the goddamn head table at the dinner tomorrow." Rasmussen breathed heavily. "It ain't fucking right!"

Michael agreed with that. *But all life is irony,* he thought. Hardee, the stupid, inept, negligent dumbjohn winds up a general officer in the United States Air Force! Christ! He regarded Rasmussen, who was drunker than he had first appeared.

"Forget him, Ras," he said.

"No way!" Rasmussen said. "No fucking way, Mike! And if you had any balls, you wouldn't forget him either!"

"Settle down, Rasmussen," Michael said sharply.

Rasmussen was immediately apologetic. "Jesus, I didn't mean that, Mike," he said. "No way!" He turned suddenly and went back into the room. The confrontation had unsettled Michael. He was tempted to leave the party. Rasmussen was clearly on his way to becoming very drunk, and he did not want to be chosen as his mentor and babysitter. Michael left the terrace and met Collins inside the door.

"Did you know that Hardee is still on active duty as a B.G.?" he asked him.

"I just heard," Collins said. "Shows you what the Air Force is coming to. Things could get nasty if he shows his face around here."

Michael saw someone steer Rasmussen into one of the side bedrooms.

"He'll be OK," Michael said.

"Gentlemen!" someone shouted. "Gentlemen!" There was the sound of a spoon being tapped against a glass.

"At ease!" someone else shouted. The room quieted gradually.

A man wearing a bright red jacket with the insignia of the 368th Squadron stood in the doorway. There were some other people whom Michael could not see.

"We have a distinguished member of the 612th visiting us!" Red Jacket shouted. "He's an old hand from the 369th, but we welcome him anyway. Brigadier General Joe Hardee, United States Air Force!" He stepped aside, and a chunky man, short, balding, and wearing an ill-fitting plaid sports jacket, green shirt, and red tie entered the main room. He held a huge cigar in his left hand and raised his right in salute.

"Carry on," Hardee said.

"Jesus!" Michael said. What devil is turning the crank, he wondered.

Daniels came up to him. "Shit!" he said. "This is crazy. Somebody better sit on Rasmussen. He was talking about popping Hardee if he ran into him."

"Can't let that happen," Collins said. He chuckled. "I never did see a brigadier general get knocked on his ass."

"I'm going to shortstop Rasmussen in the bedroom," Daniels said.

"No," Michael said. "If he comes out, he comes out."

The two men looked at Michael in surprise. Michael could not take his eyes from Hardee. He began to move toward him as if drawn by a magnet. He felt his heart begin to beat faster. Collins followed him, worried. He grabbed Michael's arm. Michael pulled away. Michael was no more than five feet from Hardee. He pushed between two men who were listening to something Hardee was saying. Then Michael was directly in front of Hardee. He said nothing. Hardee looked at him with an expression of expectancy, ready to stick out his hand. Michael did nothing, said nothing. Hardee peered at Michael's name tag.

"What's that? O'Reilly?" he said. "O'Reilly. O'Reilly. Right. Sure. I remember the name. When were you with the squadron?"

He doesn't remember, Michael thought. *The dumb bastard doesn't remember.* Michael's heart began to pound.

"I was there when you were there, Hardee," he said.

Hardee frowned at being addressed by his last name. He looked about him. But not another person was fully aware of what was going on between the two men.

"Is that right?" Hardee said. "I don't remember faces too well. The name is familiar. Sorry."

"What about Olsen?" Michael asked. "Does that ring a bell?"

Hardee became angry and turned away. Michael did not move.

"Hardee!" Michael called. He did not shout. But the sharpness of his tone stopped conversation in the immediate vicinity. Hardee stopped and turned back.

"I came here to meet old friends, O'Reilly," Hardee said. "Not to hash over old grudges. Whatever your problem is, it's yours, not mine."

Collins and Daniels had come up to flank Michael. Hardee recognized Collins immediately.

"Hello, Chip," he said. "I'd know you anywhere." He deliberately ignored Michael's presence. He looked relieved, too, expecting Collins's presence to divert Michael.

"You've got balls, Hardee," Collins said.

Michael raised his hand slightly. "This is my affair, Chip," he said. "And Rasmussen's."

"I'm here," a voice behind Michael said. He turned and saw Rasmussen, unkempt and bleary-eyed. Hardee looked frightened.

"Stay calm, Ras," Michael said.

Rasmussen raised his huge hands. He opened them wide and then clenched them into fists as Hardee stared at him. Rasmussen moved his head from side to side.

"I swore," he said. "I promised."

Other people had joined the cluster. "What is the matter?" someone asked. Nobody answered. Hardee moved back a step. Michael put his arm across Rasmussen's chest, but not hard, and Rasmussen moved it off. Rasmussen's head was steady now, and for a few seconds, his eyes were leveled at Hardee. Then he went down to his boot. He was fast but awkward from drink and rage, and Michael, after a second of indecision, reacted faster. As Rasmussen pawed at his boot for the butt of a pistol, Michael grabbed his wrist and did not let him stand up. He put his face in Rasmussen's.

"Ras! Do not do this!" Michael said. "Let it go." He squeezed his wrist harder, and Ras released his grip on the pistol. Collins reached from behind Rasmussen and pulled him up. Hardee remained frozen in place, the room quieting around him.

Rasmussen looked squarely at Michael. "What are you gonna do?" he asked him.

Michael turned and said quietly, "Hardee, you don't belong here. Get out." Hardee still didn't move. Michael suddenly stepped forward and slapped Hardee across the face with his open hand. The sound was as sharp as a gunshot and could be heard over the noisy babble of conversation. But it could have been anything. Nobody but the immediate crowd paid attention. The babble continued. Hardee did not utter a sound.

"He's a dog!" Rasmussen said. "A mutt!" He giggled. "He ain't worth shit, and he knows it." He turned away and went back to the bedroom. Michael waited. Hardee's face was flushed. His hand covered his left cheek.

"If you don't leave now," Michael said, "I'll hit you again. And

I'll keep hitting you until you leave or hit back."

"You can all go fuck yourselves," Hardee said. He turned and looked at the crowd, then pushed his way through. A woman who had heard his remark said, "Oh, my goodness!"

Michael felt no elation, no particular pride in what he had done. But he felt justified in having done it. He went to the bar and fixed himself a drink. Collins joined him.

"I don't know but that was the worst thing that could happen to that man," Collins said.

"How's Ras?" Michael asked.

"He's in there blubbering," Collins said, "but he'll be alright."

Michael and Collins crossed to the bedroom where Rasmussen was and went in.

Rasmussen was standing alone. He seemed in control of himself, no longer crying. "I guess there was no other way to do it," he said.

"Maybe," Michael said. "Maybe."

"I got a permit," Rasmussen said. "Nothing to worry about no more." He nodded his head at Michael. "I'm goin' home. I got to work tomorrow. Maybe I'll come back next year. I just don't know." Then he pushed out of the room. Nobody tried to stop him. Nobody said anything. A burst of loud laughter from the main room broke the tension in the bedroom.

"We'll walk you out," Michael said as he and Collins caught up quickly to Rasmussen.

They made their way through the room and down the elevator to the lobby. At the hotel entrance, the two men said goodbye to Rasmussen and watched him slowly walk away along the empty sidewalk.

"I'm going out where the fun is," Collins said. Michael looked at his watch. It was nearly eleven. He went back up to the hospitality suite. Emily was surrounded in one corner.

Daniels met him. "You taking off?" he asked.

"I'll see you at breakfast," Michael said.

"If you do, it'll be someone else," Daniels said. "I'm not rolling out of the rack at any eight o'clock on a Saturday morning."

Michael laughed. He was grateful that Daniels had not mentioned the Hardee incident. He went to the lobby and called Chrissie on the public telephone.

"You sound better," Chrissie said. "Have you been drinking?"

"A little," he said.

"Well, don't overdo it," she said.

"Are you coming down?" he asked.

"Yes," she said. "I'll catch the nine o'clock shuttle and be at the hotel by eleven."

"Do you want me to meet you at the airport?" he asked, surprised.

"No," she said. "I can manage. Just be careful. You sounded so down before."

"Just lonesome," he said. "I'm glad you're coming, Chris."

He thought of Emily still upstairs in the hospitality suite. He was pretty sure he could have slept with her if he had made the effort. That would be something. He tried to remember the Emily of thirty-five years ago. Vaguely, he could picture her in the private bar at The Cricketers, sipping her mild and bitter and talking intimately with Tommy Nash.

It wouldn't be the same, he told himself.

He went to the front desk for his key. "I'd like to leave a call for seven o'clock," he told the desk clerk.

"You can do that from your room," the clerk said.

The lobby was partly full of guests. It was a happy crowd. Several people smiled and spoke briefly to Michael as he walked to the elevators. He was glad he had come. Very glad.

Robert Flood was twenty-three years old when he was shot down over Germany on 29 March 1944. It had been his 25th mission, his last for that tour of duty. He would have left Europe a day or so later for home. Mind you, he had already volunteered for a second tour. He didn't want to miss the Invasion, which he and everybody knew was in the works.

Standing in the field alongside their crashed plane, Bob and his plane's pilot, Al Sheuring, watched the 8th Air Force — B-17s, just like theirs — returning to England. They cursed their bad luck and then they took off running. They didn't get very far. Local German citizens captured them and were making plans to hang them for their "crimes." Fortunately, Luftwaffe personnel arrived, overruled the angry mob, and hauled Bob and Al away. They ended up at Luft Stalag 1 in Northern Germany.

Bob remained at Stalag Luft 1 until the Russians liberated the base. Even then, it took an escape from the camp to connect with British troops and, ultimately, American command forces to finally get flown to France. Like most POWs, Bob returned to the states well after the rest of America's returning troops. No fanfare. No parades.

These stories were primarily authored 30 years after the end of the war.

Bob is our father. He didn't talk much about his WWII experience when we were kids. He would get annoyed, though, when we watched *Hogan's Heroes*. After enough time had passed, he began to speak about his experiences often ... enough. The 8th Army Air Corps reunion he attended in Washington, DC helped start that process. His participation in the National POW movement, his involvement with the 8th Air Force Museum (founding member), and his return to Luft Stalag 1 in the mid-1990s continued his ability to open up about what he'd been through.

In the last 25 years of his life, our dad lived an extraordinary journey of redemption and accomplishment. He may not have felt proud of himself when he died, but he made a difference in the lives of hundreds — maybe thousands — of veterans.

– Kevin Flood and Brian Flood.

www.ingramcontent.com/pod-product-compliance
Lightning Source LLC
Chambersburg PA
CBHW061125100726
47911CB00013B/686

* 9 7 9 8 9 9 4 2 9 5 5 1 9 *